ONE HELLUVA STORY

ONE HELLUVA STORY

KEVIN ALLEN MCKEEHAN

Cover Design: Kevin Allen McKeehan
Edited By: Leigh Anne Terry - www.latwrites.com

ONE HELLUVA STORY Copyright © 2022
by Kevin Allen McKeehan

ISBN: 979-8-9864366-0-9

First Edition: July 2022

kevinallenmckeehan@outlook.com

For my niece and nephews
Brianna, Brandon, and Brett

PROLOGUE
MARCH 31, 2018

I'd done enough research to know how to get away with murder.

I didn't think I could.

I knew I could.

I had filled my leather-bound notebook with common mistakes of murderers and serial killers who had gotten caught. They were the ones I had researched the most. I also filled my notebook with the perfect list of how to get away with murder. Each episode of true crime television provided a play-by-play list of what the killer did wrong and thus provided me a play-by-play list of what I needed to do right.

1. Ensure there was an alibi.
2. Ensure there was a great disguise.
3. Ensure no evidence was left behind.
4. Ensure the body could never be identified.

One: the alibi. I told Benjamin, my husband, I was going to Sedona for a private writing week. He knew how close I was to finishing my debut novel. He was in full agreement that a week alone was all I needed to come home with a fully completed manuscript. I had rented a room at our favorite resort he and I would often visit for quick weekend getaways. I bought tickets to go on a nighttime trail ride to search for UFOs as a reward for myself. That was not out of the ordinary for me to want to go on a UFO hunt as I always told Benjamin about the unidentified flying objects I encountered. After a few days of writing and editing, I would deserve a fun break. I did not plan on joining the tour, but I would check in on social media, saying how much fun I was having. The tour group had scheduled 27 people for that tour. I had done similar group tours before. I know I couldn't identify someone who was in any of those groups, and I was assuming no one would remember if I was there or not. It was also a 'no photos allowed' tour as the flash from the camera caused vision problems in the night, so no one on the tour would have photo evidence that I was never actually there.

Two: the disguise. Over the past three months, I had been preparing. If there was one thing I had never forgotten from one of my favorite books—"killers get caught because they are in a hurry." I purchased everything I needed with cash. I bought a short brown wig and contacts to make my eyes dark brown. I went to Walmart and purchased size 11 shoes, which were two sizes larger than my normal size. I bought ankle weights to ensure any footprints I left in the dirt would be more profound than I would typically make. It had rained yesterday, so I'm thankful I thought of this as I knew there would be tracks left in the mud. The added weight would give me—well, the detectives—the illusion of being a man much larger than I actually was. On a separate shopping trip, I purchased black leather driving gloves. I purchased bolt cutters and a new padlock in the same transaction. It seemed logical to me that if I needed to cut off a lock, I would need to replace it so I would raise no suspicion if anyone ever questioned a cashier.

I needed a large hunting knife for the weapon, one like my dad would use—one with the sharp blade on one side and the blood gutters on the other. Thankfully Walmart sold those, and thankfully my dad's birthday was coming up soon. He would be getting a slightly-used hunting knife to celebrate him turning another year older.

Three: leave no evidence. I purchased latex exam gloves on a different supply run, which I made certain were not the same brand I used at work. The next time I went shopping, I purchased tight thermal underwear, both the bottoms and the long sleeve top. They were skin-tight, which would help prevent any body hair or dead skin from falling in or around the crime scene. I had duct tape to keep all openings in the thermals closed tight. The day I planned the murder to happen, I would go get my hair cut. I always kept my hair short. A one-guard all over was what I always requested. I would carry my newly purchased jacket in with me. While the stylist cut my hair, I would leave the jacket in the waiting area. I would request a quick shampoo because I was meeting a friend for dinner and didn't want loose hairs stuck to my head. After I had my hair cut and shampooed, I would use the restroom and accidentally drop my jacket on the floor. This would cause multiple hairs from multiple people to get on the jacket. This jacket would be worn throughout the process to ensure that if any of my hair was lost at the scene, it would be in a blend of everyone else who got their hair cut that day. Statistically, only five percent of killers were caught using forensics, so the hairs on my jacket might be a little overkill, but you can never be too prepared.

Three months and 29 days ago, I told Benjamin that I would soon be finished with *She Loves Me Not*. Three months and 19 days after that, I typed The End. It wasn't quite the end, but I typed it anyway. I was so excited that six days ago I emailed a copy to both of my best friends, Marshmallow and Leigh Anne, to get their final feedback. I gave them each a deadline to get back to me in eight days. Both of them emailed me their feedback in seven. Marshmallow's feedback was in the form of a shortly worded text message. Leigh Anne's feedback was seven pages long and included a 22-slide PowerPoint! Anyone could guess whose feedback I valued more.

My debut novel had been written, read, re-written, and re-read. I was completely happy with every word that I had puzzle pieced together and every comma that I had thoughtfully typed. I was happy with the character flow. I was happy with the sketch I drew for the cover art. I was happy with my dedication and thank you pages. I was happy with the beginning, the middle, and the end. Hell, I was happy with the end of the beginning and the beginning of the end. However, I was still not happy with the murder scene. It was the only part of the story that I didn't think was believable. Leigh Anne said to leave it as is because the next step, finding an agent, would take up so much time that I needed to start pitching my book as quickly as I could. But like every other aspect of my life, I couldn't say something was finished until I loved it. I couldn't love it fully until I knew it was accurate. No amount of research would give me the real emotions someone felt when they murdered someone. I wanted to see the fear in their eyes. I wanted to feel my heartbeat accelerate. I wanted to smell the air as their soul left their body. I wanted to be the last thing they saw as they begged me to let them live.

I had thought of everything. I had everything I needed.

I, Jason Daniel Shaw, was actually going to kill someone.

CHARLI PLATT

"That cop is out there again," I said. "They've been coming around a lot more lately. I think there is a crush situation happening."

"The cute one?" Franki asked. "You know he loves me!"

"No," I said. "The other one."

My sister, Franki, and I had worked at Eight-Hundred 85 for about two months, this time around. The first time we worked here was when we were 18. It started out as a way to earn a little extra cash. Sure, our parents gave us everything we ever asked for. We were spoiled. I...we admitted that. But having our own money was different. We didn't have to tell our parents about a new dress we found or about when we threw an unusually large party in my dorm room and my dormmate's television got broken by some drunk guy. We just replaced it and didn't have to bother our parents, not that our parties were ever that crazy.

We grew up spoiled-rich-twins that everyone either admired or hated. There was no in-between when you lived in a small town. When we left for college at age 18, one of my new friends told me about Eight-Hundred 85. She said she started working there her freshman year and would bring home about $500 a night—cash.

Eventually, our family did find out, but we didn't care. At age 18, we were very good in school, and now we were also making our own money. It shocked us both when we started noticing that guys tipped more when we would dance together, a lot more. We each brought home $800 a night three nights a week. Everyone wanted to see the twins. Word got out, and eventually, we were on a billboard in the middle of Flagstaff telling everyone to come see Kendra and Blu every Wednesday, Friday, and Saturday. The day it went up, our father stopped talking to us. It took a very long time for us to fix our relationship with him. Thankfully we healed that relationship.

Franki selected the name Kendra, after her favorite character from *Buffy the Vampire Slayer*. I chose Rue after a character from my favorite book (at the time). When I told the DJ 'Rue,' he misunderstood me and announced me as Blu. I happened to wear a blue outfit that night, so the name stuck. I wore something blue from that night forward, and it became my signature.

"Ladies, it's still a packed house. Can you do another set?" the bossman asked. "I'll give you another $50 each." Julian was very selective about the girls who danced at his club. Most places would charge the girls a fee for use of their stage. Julian preferred to pay the girls a nightly wage to encourage the best of the best to represent his brand.

"Come on, Julian, we are ready to go home," I said.

"Here's another $100." He walked out of the room.

Seconds later, we heard our names. "Welcome to the stage, Kendra and Blu, the Twins."

We entranced the audience as we sauntered onto the stage and began our final final dance of the night. As usual, I entered stage left, and Franki entered stage right. There was one pole in the middle of the stage. We each ran to it, in perfect synchronization, as we had done hundreds of times before. Franki went high, and I went low. We spun in opposite directions holding on to the pole with just our thighs, mimicking a helicopter's propellers. As the momentum from the initial spin died down, we lessened our grip and slowly slid down the pole until our bodies were mirror images of each other on the floor. We released the pole, intertwined our legs, and flipped onto our stomachs. Our legs would unlock, and we would crawl in opposite directions to begin our solo performance. The crowd loved it.

After our pole routine, we went our separate ways on the stage—each of us finding the perfect person to give us their remaining cash. The bossman was right. The room was packed. I saw several new faces splashed in with the regulars. Creepy Craig was in the corner again, his hand resting in his lap under the table. Leah the Lesbian was with her five co-workers crammed into a table for two. Mysterious Michelle leaned on the wall near the exit like she had for the past three weeks. Finally, my eyes found Ten-Dollar Timmy, and I went in his direction. He loved me, and I loved his stack of ten-dollar bills. We were lucky when we got a five, but Timmy always tipped his favorite girls a ten. If you danced well enough, you could easily get $100 in five minutes from him.

I could see Franki was dancing for one of her regulars. I'd never asked his name. There was also another vaguely familiar face in the crowd. I know I had seen him here before. I remember because he looked exactly like *Cruel Intentions* era Ryan Phillippe, one of my very first crushes.

I still had the poster on my wall when I moved out of my parents' house.

He was alone. Awkward. Something just didn't seem right with him. Had he colored his hair? The lights grew brighter as we made our way off the stage.

"Don't forget, I'm leaving for Denver tomorrow," I said once we got back into the dressing room.

"Oh yea, thanks for reminding me," Franki said. "I'll swing by tonight and help you pack."

"Thanks," I said.

"I guess I'll just work alone this weekend, one sister, half the tips,"

"We can't do this forever, you know."

PART 1

ONE YEAR EARLIER

CHAPTER ONE
JASON SHAW

She Loves Me Not
First Draft

Chapter 1 - The Girl at the Grocery Store

The first time I saw her, I knew she was the one. She stared back at me for what seemed like hours, even though only a few seconds had passed. Her wavy blonde hair was pulled to each side, reminding me of ripples on a sand dune. It left a deep part down the middle. Her blue eyes were piercing, almost too painful to look at. She had a small gap between her two front teeth that made her look like one of those high fashion models on the cover of some fancy French magazine. Her Marilyn beauty mark seemed so perfectly placed that I wasn't quite sure if she had drawn it on or not. I could see why the Vista Guide picked her to be on the cover of their annual issue of "25 Under 25 Entrepreneurs in Ridgewood." I grabbed a copy of the magazine as I walked out the door—my groceries in one hand and D'Arcy Renee Chesterfield's picture in the other.

I sat in my car and quickly thumbed through the magazine until I found the article about D'Arcy. I learned she was the owner of Flower's Child, a vintage clothing store located in the heart of downtown. She was 23, single, and lived in the apartment above her store. She has a cat named Pork Chop, which I found ironic since D'Arcy is also a vegetarian. According to the article, she made $200,000 last year. That amount ranked her in the top 25 wealthiest people under the age of 25 living in the small town of Ridgewood. D'Arcy emphasized she wanted the readers to know the easiest way to remember her name is by her initials, DRC. By saying each letter individually, that's exactly how you pronounce her first name. D'Arcy explained that her mother, Rose, loved to play word games and thought it was a fun way for people to remember her daughter's name. D'Arcy joked that her future husband's last name must also begin with the letter 'C' to ensure her initials always remain the same.

My last name starts with a 'C.'

I never thought about how much personal information is in an interview, but I guess I never cared to know as much as I could about a stranger —this stranger. I also found it oddly fascinating that one could make that much money selling used clothing.

My name is Denton—Denton Maxwell Chamberlin, to be exact. I am 29 years old. I've worked as a science teacher for the past six years at the only elementary school in my town of Winchester, and I admit I love my job. I live alone in a small two-bedroom house on the outskirts of town. The house has been in my family for four generations. My great-grandfather built it for my great-grandmother the year they married. My nearest neighbor is three miles down the road. With a large wooded area between us, it almost feels as if I'm out here alone—most of the time. I've lived in the small town of Winchester my entire life. It's small enough that everyone knows me, but I don't have any close friends. I have co-workers, I have students, I have family, but I don't have friends. All in all, I'm just your average awkward guy. I blend in with the crowd and live my life day by day.

Our school's summer break started yesterday. I had bought enough groceries to last me for two weeks. I wanted these first days of break to be nothing but lazy relaxation. The last week of school is always the most stressful for a teacher; it takes almost a week to recover from the stress and excitement of the final days of the school year. This year was no exception.

I spent my first night of summer vacation tossing and turning. I could not get the image of D'Arcy's face out of my mind. I had never had a feeling so strong for another person before, let alone a person I had never even spoken with. I silently said my nightly prayer and decided to go to Flower's Child the next day.

"Thank you God for sending me an angel," I said.

Sleep came quickly after I made my decision, and morning came even faster. I woke, as usual, at 5:47 a.m. I have an irrational fear of even numbers. They always seem to bring me bad luck. It's called "omalonumerophobia." I was born on 11/23/75. All odd. My time of birth: 5:17 p.m., all odd. I weighed 7lbs, 7oz. My mother's recovery room after my birth, 351. There are 23 letters in my full name. Odd. Odd. Odd. I've heard the whispers in the halls from my co-workers, they also say I'm odd.

Odd.

I started the coffee pot, made myself some breakfast, and turned on the news. I've always prided myself on keeping up-to-date with current affairs. Living in such a small town, I must stay prepared for the inevitable day-to-day small talk. I quickly showered and then stood staring in my closet for my most vintage-looking shirt. I knew my future wife would appreciate my clothing choice. I decided on a red plaid button-down. It had trims of tan suede on the cuffs, the pocket, and the collar. I paired it with my favorite faded jeans and finished the look with a denim jacket trimmed with faux fur. Yes, it was probably too warm today to be wearing a fur-lined jacket, but what the hell. I knew D'Arcy would appreciate it. I poured the last of my coffee in a travel mug, grabbed my copy of the Vista Guide, and began my 45-minute drive to Ridgewood.

As I got closer to the city limit, I typed the address to D'Arcy's shop into my phone's navigation. As always, the voice gave me turn-by-turn directions. My heart began to beat faster. "In one mile, turn right onto Jackson Street." In one mile, I followed my orders. "In 300 feet, turn left onto Cherry Lane." In 300 feet, I turned left. "Continue on Cherry Lane for one mile, and your destination will be on your right." And just like that, I pulled into a parking space directly in front of Flower's Child.

I sat there for 17 minutes looking through the window. The early morning sun glared brightly on the glass, showing the reflection of the buildings behind me and making it almost impossible to see inside. I checked my hair in my mirror—it's still there! Dark. Neatly combed. Every strand in its place. My perfectly manicured hands reached to open the door of my car. I headed towards my destiny.

CHAPTER TWO
JASON SHAW

Leigh Anne and I sat talking like we did every Wednesday. We had been friends since the first day we met at work many, many years ago in a rundown taco shop in a dying part of town. I do have to say we were the best damn burrito rollers you have ever met. Nice and tight. Dare I say it? OK, fine, that's what she said! Sure, we did things other than just roll burritos. We filled taco shells, piled toppings on nachos, and put ice in the cup before filling it with your soda choice. We did all of the not so difficult tasks that came with working at a taco shop. "Bueno, Bonito, y Barato" and their lackluster Taco Tuesdays was where these two amigos became best friends.

Those days were long gone. Leigh Anne was now a published author and a personal chef to the stars. Well, the "wannabe" Real Housewives of Paradise Valley. Trust me; they didn't eat burritos. I doubt Leigh Anne's Taco Tuesday training had been helpful for any of those women.

Leigh Anne's novels were excellent, in my opinion. They were a continual series about Tomas Randy, a rough and tough, shoot 'em up, time travelin' cowboy. His sole purpose in life was to save his girlfriend from the bad guys. I still laugh every time she would tell me how the damsel in distress got into distress in each new book. Oh, yes, I've read them all! One of the perks of being Leigh Anne's best friend was getting to read her book as she wrote it. I got the inside scoop on where Tomas' time-traveling adventures would take him before anyone else got to know!

I was the owner of The Golden Bones. It was a retirement home for unwanted, unloved, and sometimes sick senior pets. I say retirement home, but it was more of a mix between a retirement home and a hospice for your furry friends. My business card actually said, "In dog years, I'm retired."

When our burrito rolling days were over, Leigh Anne and I made a pact to meet every Wednesday to ensure the continuation of our friendship. We've all had those work friends who said, "I'll keep in touch!" Two weeks after you have quit your job, they might as well have been complete strangers. You send a random text to say "Hi," and only get a one-word reply. When anyone ever sent me a one-word text, I assumed our conversation was over. And do not get me started with a text that just says, "Hey." My friend Alex does that all the time. You always remain Facebook friends and offer up a "like" here and there, but the friendship eventually died. I hated it when that happened.

Anyway, Leigh Anne and I made a pact not to become "those people." Aside from a legitimate excuse here and there for not being able to meet, we have gotten together every Wednesday. And yes, we had a list of 22 legitimate excuses that allowed for a Wednesday cancellation.

1. Car accident (Only one involving her or me. You could be late due to a car accident of others slowing you down, but you couldn't cancel).

2. Your dog ran away, and you have to look for them.

3. You or anyone you know was abducted by aliens.

4. Explosive diarrhea or Exorcist-style projectile vomiting (both required photo evidence).

The list went on and on.

Sometimes we spent our weekly encounter having coffee, sometimes it was devouring tacos, and sometimes it was just sitting on a park bench with handheld paper fans to keep us cool. Today, we enjoyed mimosas on my back porch—fresh squeezed orange juice mixed with True Colors cava.

Today, I specifically invited Leigh Anne over to read the first few pages of the book I was attempting to write, *She Loves Me Not*. At least, that was what I thought I would call it, eventually. It was the fifth title I'd come up with, and I cannot guarantee it will be the last. It was the story of D'Arcy and Denton. At this moment, it was going to be a stalker love story because of my love for true crime shows. Guy meets girl, girl thinks guy is crazy, guy kidnaps girl, and they fall in love and live happily ever after. But, I had never written a book. For all I knew, it could be guy meets girl, girl says leave me alone, and guy leaves the girl alone —the end.

Through the continued "How to Write a Novel" research I had been doing, I had come to understand the characters wrote their own story. Leigh Anne, the one who inspired me to write, had told me many times, "Jason, no matter how much you think you know what will happen, the characters tell you how they will live their lives." Do not get me started on all the research I had done. My husband once told me if I spent as much time writing the book as I had spent researching how to write a book, it would be completed, published, and I would be writing my third new novel by now. He was not wrong! I think I loved researching almost as much as I loved my new writing hobby. I was able to put on paper all of the things I was afraid to do in real life.

"You are one of the lucky ones who has two jobs that you love," I said. "Writing and cheffing, two hobbies that you made into lucrative careers."

"Cheffing?" she laughed.

"Yes, cheffing," I said. "The act of being a chef."

"Use it in a sentence," she said.

"Yesterday, while cheffing for Tiffani, two *i*'s, with hearts, not dots, I prepared a delicious and healthy meal that she enjoyed," I said matter-of-factly.

An immediate eye roll from Leigh Anne occurred.

As I understood it, my life was the life of your average man. I was married. I worked 40+ hours a week. I had three dogs, two tortoises, and a fish tank that housed four very aggressive angelfish. Tortoises was a dumb plural word, I agree. I wish it were "torti." I did know that a group of tortoises was called a creep, but I wasn't sure how many made a group. Maybe I actually had a creep of tortoises?

I had recently turned 41 years old, yesterday in fact. I was at that age when I talked about my 20s, it seemed like they were only five years ago. I always enjoyed a good "that's what she said" joke (see the earlier part of this chapter for reference).

I changed my hobbies about every six months hoping to find the one thing I loved that would allow me to share my creative side with the world. You know the saying, "I'm just throwing noodles at the wall until something sticks?" Well, that was me. Over the past five years, I had learned to brew beer and make homemade butter and cheese—not all at the same time. I'd taught myself how to make soaps, potions, and lotions. I had carved walking sticks from broken trees and learned to make belts from the skins of rattlesnakes I have killed while hiking through the desert. That was just a small list of my favorite things to do from specific points in my life.

I secretly hoped to find a hobby that would make me famous. Not just Instagram famous, real-life famous. Some have said that I can't stay focused on one thing, while others have said I have commitment issues and can't follow through with things I start. Who? Well, my father, my niece, my husband, and I can't forget Leigh Anne! I always completed all projects I started. Well, most of them. I still have an unfinished quilt in my closet. Quilting was not my thing! Attempting to write a book was my newest "favorite thing" project. I didn't think the world was ready for me, Jason, the next author that would be all over #bookstagram! OK, fine. I would be happy just being Instagram famous. I already had 154 followers, so I was well on my way.

Deep down, I knew the real reason I didn't always finish my projects was my fear of rejection. If I never finished the painting, no one could tell me they didn't like it. If I never finished the quilt, no one could say to me it could have been better. If I never finished my book, I would never have to read comments from people who hated it.

I sat there watching the lack of expression on Leigh Anne's face as she read chapter one of my attempt at

10

writing what I hoped would become an Amazon Top 100 bestseller. I tried not to stare while she read to make it less uncomfortable for both of us. It took me months to come up with an idea for my book. When I gave Leigh Anne the basic synopsis, she smiled. She's been writing for 15 years, some freelance work here, an article there, and her claim to fame—the adventures of Tomas. Her opinion was crucial to me and the future of my book. She was the only friend of mine who would tell it like it is. She sat down the pages when she finished reading.

"What do you think?" I asked.

She looked me directly in the eyes and said, "Have you ever picked up a book, read a few lines, and set it down? It happens to me all the time. The hook isn't there. It's just blah. With this," she said as she held up my pages, "I'm interested. I'm curious. I'm excited to read more. You've been talking about this book for weeks now. I'm glad it has started to take its shape."

With that comment, I was excited to continue on the path of writing my first book.

CHAPTER THREE
SHE LOVES ME NOT

Chapter 2 — Our First Date

DAY ONE:

"Hello, welcome to Flower's Child," she said as she did with everyone who walked into the shop. Since the article in the Vista Guide had been published, she had been saying it a lot. Flower's Child had always been the local go-to shop for vintage clothing, but now it is a destination for many who have just shopped from the sidewalk and those who would only peer in and continue to pass by.

D'Arcy has been the owner of Flower's Child for the past 13 months. She'd always dreamed of owning her own business. Knowing her dream and her love of fashion, D'Arcy's parents bought a used clothing store as her high school graduation present. They told her they would not hand over the keys until she held her college diploma. That diploma now hangs in her store.

D'Arcy's mother, Rose, ran the shop while D'Arcy was in college. It was never a hotspot for used clothing while Rose was in charge. It managed to make enough revenue to keep the doors open without causing any financial burden on the family.

D'Arcy is a smart girl. Armed with the marketing knowledge she was gaining in school, she utilized the power of the internet. With help from her best friend, Stevie, she started an Instagram account. Stevie was a good amateur photographer. The two of them would do photoshoots almost every weekend. D'Arcy's stunning looks and her fashion sense combined with the artistic photography gained thousands of followers in a short amount of time. By the time D'Arcy completed her degree and took the reins from her mother, Flower's Child had a huge internet following. Once D'Arcy was in charge of every aspect of the business, she began to sell online as well as in the store. Flower's Child became a success. It was a fine example of what determination, when combined with an excellent education, can do.

"My sister read the article and couldn't stop talking about how much she loved your style. Can you help me pick out an outfit for her?" I asked as I held up my copy of Vista Guide.

"I would love to help you," she said. "I'm D'Arcy. What's your name?"

"Denton," I said. "Denton Chamberlin."

We spent the next 15 minutes walking around the store and talking about clothes. I had no interest in the clothes at all. I only wanted to stare at her while she spoke. We picked out an outfit, and I left the store. I sat in my car for at least an hour, catching small glimpses of her through the store windows as she went about her day. I left my parking spot and instantly knew I wanted to see her again.

DAY TWO:

D'Arcy woke at 8:00 a.m. That's when she usually starts her day. Her apartment is above the shop. It never takes her more than a minute to get to work. She usually arrives at the shop at 9:00 a.m., does the morning paperwork, the banking, and opens the doors precisely at 10:00 a.m. During the weekdays, D'Arcy is usually alone in the shop until noon; that's when Stevie comes in. Stevie works in the store and is fully responsible for all social media accounts. She happens to be the only other employee who works at Flower's Child.

Over the weekend, customers brought several new items into the store. Clothing that they had sold, donated, or exchanged for store credit to use towards other items for themselves. Today was the day that D'Arcy would get all of those items laundered, pressed, hung, and priced.

One of the things D'Arcy does differently that sets her apart from the competition is she washes and irons each item of clothing that comes into the store. She loves the vintage style but hates the vintage smell that you notice when you walk in other second-hand clothing stores. You know the one—musty mothballish, mixed with southern humidity on a hot day. Flower's Child smells like dryer sheets and fresh-cut wildflowers. A massive bouquet always sits on the table in the center of the store. I could see from my car that today's flowers were stargazer lilies, bright pink petals contrasting against their dark green stems. Beauty in a jar, beauty in a store.

The bell that hangs above the door rang at 10:07 a.m. alerting her that the first customer had arrived. That customer happened to be me. I had been sitting in my car for one hour and nineteen minutes.

"Welcome back," she said. "I hope your sister was happy."

I was excited that she remembered me.

"She was, however, the size was wrong," I replied. "We need something a little smaller. How was the rest of your evening?"

"Nothing special," she said. "I had a nice relaxing evening alone after work."

"How can you be alone when you have Pork Chop?" I asked with a mischievous smile.

"Ahh, so you must have read the article, too," she said. "That article was a blessing and a curse. Business has picked up a lot since it was published, but it seems everyone who walks in now knows many things that once were only known to a select few." She started mindlessly refolding some jeans that were on a table.

I could tell she enjoyed talking to me.

"But listen to me ramblin' on," she continued. "Let's find your sister something smaller."

Ramble on? Did she say ramble on? I only heard a few sentences. I must have been captivated by her smile. Her beauty mark was still there. Just as perfectly placed as the first time I saw it.

She and I walked the store once again, almost like it was our second date. My body shivered when our hands brushed as she handed me the bag with my sister's clothes.

"Thanks for coming back, I hope these work out better for you, well for your sister," she said with a smile. "Have a fantastic day, and we'll see you soon!"

See me soon? What does that mean? Does she want me to come back tomorrow? I put my bag in the trunk of my car, next to the bag of clothes I purchased yesterday. I did some window browsing at the adjacent shops and turned back to head towards my car. My car, once again, happened to be parked in front of Flower's Child. I stood next to my car, looking into the store where my beloved continued to work.

DAY THREE:

"I was in the neighborhood," I said. "Can you recommend a place for me to take my Nana to lunch?" Today's reason to stop by the shop was a little off the wall, I know, but I didn't care.

"I'm so sorry," she said. "What was your name again?" The tone in her voice was a little harsh.

"Denton, Denton Chamberlin."

"Well, Denton Chamberlin, I can honestly say you have been my most frequent customer this week," she said. "Are you new in town?"

"No," I said. "I'm from Winchester. I'm an elementary school science teacher, and it's summer break. I usually spend my summers alone in my home, but I wanted this year to be different. This summer, I decided to spend it exploring the area. I've lived in Winchester my whole life and rarely make it to Ridgewood. There are so many places I've never been to. I try to support local businesses, and since you are a local business owner, I thought you might be able to recommend a great place for me and my nana to eat. I'm sorry if I am taking up your time." I turned to walk out.

Listen to me; now I'm the one rambling.

She stopped me from leaving and gave me her recommendation. I politely thanked her and smelled the flowers on the table, I got pollen on my nose. I brushed at it and quickly left the store, unsure if I cleaned it off or made it worse. D'Arcy stood near the window and watched me walk away. She rechecked the clock just as the bell above the door rang. It was Stevie. She told her about Denton and the creepy vibe he was giving off. The two of them quickly went into the office and pulled up the video from the security camera to see if Stevie recognized him.

"Nope, never seen him before," Stevie said. "He's cute. If he comes back, give him my number." She said the last part with a high pitched laugh punctuating her statement.

"Shut up," D'Arcy said. "The strange thing is, well, one of the strange things, he asked for a recommendation for a place to take his Nana to eat, yet when he got in his car, there was no one in it."

"That is strange," said Stevie. "Maybe he is on his way to pick her up?"

"The car was a navy blue Chevy Cruze, just in case I go missing," D'Arcy said as she winked at Stevie.

"If you go missing, can I have the store?" Stevie asked.

DAY FOUR:

I drove around the block three times before parking my car. The first time around the block, I discovered an alley that ran behind the shop. Some stairs led from the back door to an apartment that was above Flower's Child. Remembering the article where I first met D'Arcy said she lived above her store, I knew this had to be her home. The second time around the block, I saw a cat sitting in the window of that apartment. The third time around the block was to ensure I drove around it an odd number of times.

Odd.

I parked my car and walked into the store. She wasn't there. I had a large bag of items in my hands and thought it would look weird if I didn't talk to the associate.

"My Nana was cleaning out her closet," I said. "Are you interested in any of these things?"

I stood there trying to read the expression on her face. It was a look of excitement, nervousness, and a little anxiety. I knew instantly that D'Arcy had told her about me and my visits, but how did she know it was me? I could only imagine that D'Arcy was saying great things about me. Maybe this is a sign that it's time to ask her out.

The associate took the bag and said she would look through it in the backroom. "There's more space for me to lay things out and examine them," she said. "I'll be right back to let you know what I can take."

Stevie took the bag into the back, but didn't sort through the clothes; she grabbed her cell phone and text D'Arcy.

I think that man is here again; she pressed send.

OH MY GOD; D'Arcy wrote back.

I left before she came from the back. I wasn't interested in the money she might have offered for the bag of clothes. The clothes were not even my Nana's. They were items I picked up from the Goodwill on my way to Flower's Child this morning.

I drove to the grocery store and picked out a small bouquet of fresh flowers. I signed the card with "See you soon." I drove back toward D'Arcy's apartment. I parked on a nearby street and headed up the stairs.

I knocked on the door three times. Not two and not four. I waited. After no response, I left the flowers on the landing outside her door.

Odd.

DAY FIVE:

D'Arcy had barely flipped the sign to say Open and gotten the doors unlocked when I pushed through the door, tinkling the little bell to announce my arrival. "I know it may seem like I'm obsessing, but I can't stop thinking about you," I said. "Would you like to have dinner sometime?" I knew the expression on my face was probably concerning because I am not very good at asking girls out. I always get rejected, but I never lose hope.

"Denton, I only know the names of two types of customers that come in my store," she said. "One: those who are frequent and are great customers that I look forward to seeing; and two: those who are always in here complaining about something. 'This shirt costs too much.' 'The price tag is missing from these shoes. They must be free!' You have now forced me to create a third reason to remember someone's name—people who think they know me and drive 45 minutes each day to stalk me. I have to say no to your date and also ask that you please stop coming into my store."

I could feel the look of anger forming on my face. I turned quickly to break the stare and exited the building. My rejection success rate continues. This time, I will not give up so easily. Maybe she needs time to miss me. I mean, we have been together for the past five days. Not four. I am still counting the day with Stevie as a day with D'Arcy.

Five days.

Odd.

I got in my car and drove around to the back. I parked in the alley and waited for the store to close just so I could see her climb the stairs to her apartment. I wanted to see her one more time before I went home.

DAY SIX:

I couldn't leave my house. After my failed attempt at securing a date I was embarrassed. I was humiliated. I was pissed. What was it about me that she didn't like? I mean, it was just a simple dinner. It's not like I asked her to marry me.

I opened my laptop and searched the internet for a florist. It was the first time I had opened my laptop in a long time. It took a while for it to load. I selected an arrangement of wildflowers. I entered the address of D'Arcy's store and typed "forgive" as the single word message to be on the card. I left my name off the card.

I had spent the entire week watching D'Arcy. No, I was learning D'Arcy. I learned her schedule. I learned what time she went to lunch. I learned what time she went on her breaks. I learned what time she went to her apartment. This week I learned a lot.

DAY SEVEN:

5:45 p.m.

In 15 minutes D'Arcy will walk to the door and flip the Open sign to Closed. She will lock the two locks on the front door and twist the stick on the blinds to shut them. She will walk to the cash register, remove the money, and walk to the shop's backroom. At 6:15 p.m. she will exit the shop through the back door and ascend the staircase to her apartment. I've watched the process happen three times through the storefront windows. Tonight, I will be watching the process from the alley behind the buildings. I left a rose with no card attached at the top of the stairs to show her how much I care.

As expected, she came out the back, climbed the stairs, and picked up the rose. I expected a smile to form on her face. I hoped that even in the dim evening light, I would see the sparkle in her blue eyes, telling me that she loves me.

She ripped the petals off the stem and tossed them over the rails. As the last one hit the ground, she loves me not.

CHAPTER FOUR
JASON SHAW

It was Wednesday, and I got to pick our meeting place this week. This week I chose to meet at the park near my house. It had a huge duck pond. I recently read an article about not feeding ducks bread and wanted to take a gander at the article's other recommendations. The article said bread had no nutritional value. It only filled up the duck's stomach and made them not want to eat other things. I learned that when I fell down an internet rabbit hole while researching something completely unrelated, as I often did. I packed the ducks a can of corn, a can of peas, and a small bag of dried oats. Thank God for pull-top canned goods!

Leigh Anne and I would be snacking as well. We would have the cupcakes I had made the previous night in honor of Dolly Parton's birthday. Along with the cupcakes, we each had individual boxes of red wine.

"I'm having a hard time writing in order," I said. "I get an idea in my head and jot down little notes. But when it comes to writing the part I had written about in my notes, I forget what I really wanted to write in the first place!"

"Who said you have to write in order?" Leigh Anne asked. "Write what you know and what you feel when you know it and when you feel it. You have plenty of time to go back, edit, re-write, and rearrange." She paused. "And trust me, you will go back, edit, re-write, and rearrange."

"I know, but…" I wasn't sure how to finish that sentence.

"And speaking of your notes," she said as she reached into her bag. "I got you this." Leigh Anne handed me a leather-bound notebook. It was dark brown leather and had gold letters stamped on the front reading 'Author's Notes.'

"Oh my God," I said. "This is beautiful." I sat there flipping through the blank pages and taking in the smell. Woody, earthy, vanilla. Addictive.

"You're welcome! It is small enough to carry around with you, yet large enough to keep you using it for a very long time. I find it's more meaningful to write on paper than to jot a quick note in your phone or on your screen. It makes you think about what you want to remember. I enjoy going through my old journals to see what things I wrote down on paper actually made it into my finished projects.

"There have been times when I spent just as much time on the editing and rearranging phase as I have on the initial writing. Everyone has a different style of writing, and no one style is the right style," she said.

"I will treasure it forever," I said as I placed the journal in my lap. "What's your feedback for today?"

"It's pretty straightforward," she said. "Sometimes you speak in the present tense, and sometimes you speak in the past tense, but that's an easy fix. More importantly, you're getting lost in who is telling the story."

"OK, for example...?"

"For example," she said, "Denton is the main character and the one telling the story, right?"

"Yes," I said.

"Perfect, then we are on the same page," she said. "When Denton is in the store, he's telling the story, and then he leaves. Since he's telling the story and he's no longer in the store, there shouldn't be any way he knows the dialogue happening between D'Arcy and Stevie."

"That makes sense," I said. "I guess I'll do some of that so-called 'editing' you were speaking of. What about the present versus past tense? Which one is better?"

"Oh, I can't answer that for you. You gotta pick one and stick to it, but you had past, present, and future on one page."

I glanced at the edge of the pond and noticed corn kernels all over the ground. The peas had either been eaten or secretly hidden like I would do with mine when I was a kid.

"It appears ducks like the canned peas most of all," I said.

"I wonder if a duck dish with a side of peas would be good?" Leigh Anne asked.

"Sounds like a cheffing adventure is about to happen," I said.

She peered off into the distance as if she were thinking of a long-lost love. I knew she was thinking of food. I got that same look in my eyes when I knew she was going to cook for me. She was quite pretty when she was lost in thought. Well, I guess she was quite pretty all the time. But, when she was in her food daydreams, her brown eyes sparkled like a cold bowl of chocolate pudding.

"I've decided to kill D'Arcy," I said. That quickly shook her out of her mind's prep kitchen.

"That's an unexpected turn of events," Leigh Anne said.

"You told me the characters write their own story," I said. "Denton told me he wants to kill her. But more than just kill her—crucify her."

She looked at me with a mix of confusion and understanding. I didn't know that was a thing until now.

"Ahh, they are talking to you now," she said. "I wish the three of you the best of luck. I'm curious as to how that will play out."

We sat there, snacked on our snacks, drank our adult juice boxes, and talked about fun ways to murder someone. None of the passersby seemed to overhear, and if they did, they must have been too afraid to comment or look our way.

CHAPTER FIVE
SHE LOVES ME NOT

Chapter XX

[author's note: add this section after Denton kills D'Arcy]

I stood there watching the countdown.

00:05

I knew I had just changed my life forever.

00:04

I knew I had just changed the life of D'Arcy's family forever.

00:03

Why did I feel no remorse?

00:02

What will happen if someone finds out?

00:01

I quickly reached up and opened the microwave before the annoying alarm alerted my empty house that my dinner was warm. Tonight's feast was meatloaf covered in a red ketchup-like sauce, kernels of yellow corn soaking in cloudy water, and a square pile of what was supposed to be mashed potatoes with an unmelted pat of butter sitting on the top. Why that pat of butter never melts I will never understand. I grabbed my microwaved meal, sat down in my living room, and turned on the TV. It was 5:30 p.m. and the Channel 3 news was just starting. Thursday night's news segments: more rain this weekend, the Humane Society is holding a discounted pet adoption on Friday, and a Ridgewood business owner is still missing.

If at least one person knows where you are, then you can never really be missing. I know precisely where the Ridgewood business owner is, so technically she's not missing. She's dead. Her cold body is laying in my back yard in the exact spot I left her three days ago. I was hoping some hungry animal from the woods would come and drag her off, and I wouldn't have the burden of disposing of her. At least the wet earth will make it easier to dig the grave.

I woke early on Friday and drove into town. I'd never owned a pet before, but today would be the day that changed. I wanted the biggest dog I could find. A guard dog. A protector. I entered the Humane Society and walked the aisle between rows of caged, barking dogs. It didn't take me long to find a large male pit mix. The sign on his cage said his owner relinquished him. He was great with children, but he didn't like other animals. His name was Bruce. He was four years old. He was exactly what I was looking for. I filled out the exhausting amount of paperwork and handed over the advertised discounted adoption fee of $50.

Bruce sat in the front with me on the ride home. His tail wagged and his lips flapped wildly as he stuck his head out the window. I've always heard dogs like cheeseburgers, so I decided to pick one up for Bruce on the way to his new home.

Yesterday, I walked 97 paces into the woods behind my house and dug a grave for the shop owner. I placed her in the dampened earth. I filled only half of the grave with dirt. Today, Bruce and I retraced my steps to that grave. He needed to see what he would be guarding for me. I threw the now cold drive-thru cheeseburger into the grave. He quickly jumped in after it. Bruce ate the entire thing in 2 bites.

Then, I shot him.

I buried man's best friend and went back to the house to wash the mud off my shovel. One of my earliest memories of my father was cleaning, sharpening, and oiling his shovel after every use. "That's why this shovel is 15 years old and still looks new," he'd always told me.

* * *

"OK, stop right there," Leigh Anne said.

We were sitting at Wing and a Prayer enjoying wings and fries. Leigh Anne was reading my draft, and I was dipping fries in the buffalo sauce that had pooled on my plate.

"You can't just go buy a dog and kill him on the same page," she said as she chewed a handful of fries she had just shoved in her mouth. "You shouldn't even kill a dog! People get upset when pets and children die in books and movies, as you know."

"But you see, when or if the cops come to search the land, they will see the grave. Their instinct will be that D'Arcy is there, so what will they do? Start to dig," I said.

"And then they will find a dog buried in the grave and stop their digging," Leigh Anne said. Her expression was that of delight. She had finally swallowed her mouthful of fries.

She continued reading, and I sat on my phone. Let me rephrase that. I didn't actually sit on my phone. I sat, playing on my phone. "See Jason, commas are important. Words are important. You are building worlds for strangers to enter. Your fingers are molding their imagination." I could hear Leigh Anne's voice in my head, although I'm sure she would not say the last part.

* * *

Did you know that you never forget a face? Your brain stores the information of every person

32

that you encounter in your day-to-day activities. The people you see in your dreams are just the faces of those you have passed throughout your lifetime; the person at the mall, a passenger in a car you passed, maybe an extra in the background of a movie. They can all appear in your dreams.

I've always wondered about the monsters in my dreams. Are they things I have encountered in my day-to-day activities too? Were they hiding in plain sight or were they disguised as people? Did the dream world pull off their disguise to allow their true identity to show?

Last night, for the first time in many months, the demons were in my dreams. When I was a kid and would wake from a nightmare, my mom would ask me to tell her exactly what happened in my dream. She told me to change the ending to something happy and not scary. Last night I didn't have a nightmare. Dark figures were standing in the woods near my house. They had never stood there before. I don't know how to change the end of that dream to make it happy just yet.

[author's note: these two paragraphs need something to join them more cohesively. Maybe add some connection about demons and mental health?]

I'm lonely again. The shopkeeper had occupied my time and my mind for the past three weeks, and now she had abandoned me. I still talked to her as if she were sitting next to me. I did keep a small lock of her hair to help me remember her smell.

A single blonde wavy lock.

A lock that would forever be missing it's key.

CHAPTER SIX
CHARLI PLATT

"What are you girls going to do now that you are grown up?" my Aunt Alice asked.

"I don't think a college degree makes either of us a grown-up!" Franki said. She built another burger from the buffet my mom and dad had prepared—bun, patty, ketchup, onion, bun.

"Franki didn't even go to class the last three months, Aunt Alice," I said. "So, I know she's not a grown-up. I started applying at a few papers in Flag, but I might try TV as well."

Mom peeked around the corner, "You know I can hear you, right? You girls should not have been skipping class!"

"It wasn't me!" I replied.

Franki and I laughed. Our graduation party was the first time we'd had a big gathering at our house in a very long time. Mom was always the first to say, "Let's have a party," for any event. After the disastrous Sweet 16 party, my mom said no to every other party occasion.

"I'm heading to Phoenix," Franki said. "It's time to spread my wings."

"Why Phoenix?" Aunt Alice asked.

"I went down there last summer with a friend. She's from there," Franki said. "We stayed in her parents' winter home. They're snowbirds. I loved it. I worked a little that summer, met some people, made some friends, and really liked it."

"She also got herself a stalker," I said.

"What?" Aunt Alice gasped.

"It was nothing, Auntie," Franki said. "It was just a guy who was misinterpreting signs. He thought I liked him. I thought he was normal, the usual story with me. But it really was no big deal."

"She had to get the cops involved," my mom said. "But it was no big deal," my mom said, making air quotes around no big deal.

"Anything involving the cops is a big deal, dear," Aunt Alice said.

"She thought it was a big deal when she got home that fall, Alice," Mom said.

"Why did you never tell me about this?" Aunt Alice asked my mom.

"The police advised us to keep it quiet at the time. So that's what we did."

My mom began to fill Aunt Alice in on the event while Franki and I made the rounds to socialize with the rest of the guests.

"Phoenix? Again? Really?" I asked. "You haven't mentioned that in a long time."

"I know, I'm just afraid if I stay here this summer, it will turn into another summer and then another summer after that," Franki said. "Before you know it, me and you are old women setting up a burger buffet for our daughters, and we never explored the world!"

"I know. It was just a shock to hear," I said.

"Don't you want to see the world?" she asked.

I could still hear my mom and aunt talking in the other room. Those ladies don't know the meaning of not telling the whole family our family secrets.

"That's one helluva story," Aunt Alice said.

CHAPTER SEVEN
JASON SHAW

"I'm having a hard time sleeping lately," I said to my husband.

"It's probably all that crazy stuff you are looking up online about murder," Benjamin replied.

"I just want my book to be something that I'm proud of, and I will only be proud if I know the things I write are as accurate as possible," I said.

I guess I would have to start hiding my research from my husband and tell him I was reading articles on things such as urban gardening or how to teach a parrot to talk. Light bulb moment! That was what I was looking up when I found out not to feed ducks bread!

Benjamin had expressed zero interest in reading my book. I could have very well been researching urban gardening. Maybe in the next chapter, Denton would move into the city and leave his farmland behind. He might need to know how to grow a windowsill herb garden.

I had written the murder scene two times, but I can't seem to make it sound realistic. I had read every online tip that I could find about how to write a murder scene. They all said the same things. My theory was if every article I read online was telling me the same thing, then it must be true. Either that or it must be the most fundamental way to put down the steps that occurred when you killed someone.

I read multiple interviews with convicted murderers and serial killers to see if their words would inspire me. The research led me to conclude that there were many people in the world that you never knew you should have been afraid of. I wondered what it would be like. What emotion would a person feel? Would it be something that was recognizable?

The research always showed that there was usually one tiny detail that someone overlooked. It could be something as small as why an animal lover killed rattlesnakes, or maybe the detective didn't notice that in the back of the boyfriend's truck was a seedpod from a tree that only grew in the exact region where the victim's body was dumped. You know, something small like that. When someone finally discovered that detail, you had your killer.

What mistake will Denton make? I needed to think about that, that is, if I decided to let him get caught.

What mistake would I make?

* * *

SHE LOVES ME NOT

[authors note: add chapter numbers and chapter titles once the book is completed and organized in chronological order]

Chapter XX

She stood there, trembling. I couldn't tell if she was scared or furious. I hoped it was fear. I had never made a woman tremble before. The emotion I was seeing in her face, that fear, was making me excited in a strange way. I wasn't prepared for what happened next.

"If you do not leave I will shoot you Denton," D'Arcy said. "I've told you many times to leave me alone. Stop sending me flowers and stop coming to my store. Leave me the hell alone! I'm serious!"

"D'Arcy, you've got to understand," I pleaded. "I can't live without you. You are my soul mate. We're meant to be together."

She reached into a drawer under the cash register, pulled out a gun, and shot me in the leg. It burned, both my leg and my love for her.

"I warned you Denton," she said. "Get out!"

I limped to my car, slowly losing blood from the small hole in my lower leg. She didn't want to kill me. She only wanted to scare me so much that I knew to leave her alone forever. D'Arcy is not one of the helpless women you usually find in the story-books. She was a strong independent woman who wouldn't take anything from any man. [author's note: show me, don't tell me! How is she a strong woman?]

I was still able to drive and went to the ER. I told the doctor that I had been cleaning my gun for a weekend camping trip I had planned when it accidentally went off. The doctor didn't seem alarmed by my story. She cleaned the wound, added a few small stitches, and sent me on my way.

[author's note: do some quick research on bullet wounds to see if the above is accurate and to verify if doctors have to report bullet wounds. Leigh Anne says you do. Also, did that scene happen too fast?]

I sat in the hospital parking lot replaying the look of fear in D'Arcy's eyes. I couldn't help but feel angry about how the look in her eyes turned from fear to strength. I didn't like the look of strength. How could I be the provider for someone who could provide for herself already? I also can't understand how she could so easily shoot me just to prove a point.

But she didn't kill me—that means she cares.

I drove back to the scene of the crime. The closed sign was already on the store's door. The blinds were closed.

Any other day I knew she would be in her apartment 10 minutes after the store was closed. I had her routine memorized. At 6:00 p.m. she would lock the door, do the paperwork for the night and then head upstairs to her apartment. I had watched the actions every day for the last 4 days.

She was supposed to lock the shop, walk up the stairs, and find a rose laying on the top step. She would then unlock her apartment door and find me in her kitchen holding more roses. She would have to say yes to a date. Today's encounter messed with my plans.

I parked my car, went upstairs and turned the doorknob. The door was unlocked. She must be home. I slowly opened the door and let myself in. Her apartment was nice. Everything was in it's place. Neat. Organized. I walked into her living room.

Where was she?

"How did you get into my apartment?" she yelled.

"D'Arcy, I just needed you to see that we are meant to be together, God sent you to me." I said. "If I have the gift of prophecy and can fathom all mysteries and all knowledge, and if I have a faith that can move mountains, but do not have love, I am nothing. [author's note: 1 Corinthians 13:2] I am nothing without you."

She started running towards a drawer near the kitchen where I was standing; she quickly pulled it open and pulled out a gun. [author's note: does she own too many guns? Might need to explain that at some point] I was suddenly forced to do something that was not part of the plan. I hit her. I hit her so hard that my knuckles instantly began to bleed. She fell down in the doorway between the kitchen and her living room.

She can't say no to me now. I smiled.

I stood there waiting for her to get up. But she didn't. I couldn't leave her alone. I picked her up, carried her down the stairs, and sat her in the backseat of my car. I quickly ran back up to D'Arcy's place and ensured everything was put back in its place. I closed the drawer the gun was in, picked up the rose she stepped over when she entered her place, and locked the door behind me. It was as if she never came home.

I took her cell phone from her back pocket. I would have to toss that out of the window on the drive home and hope it was never found.

It started to rain on the drive to my home—our home. I love the rain. It is nature's way of cleaning the earth. My mother always told me there are those who walk in the rain and those who just get wet. I don't think she came up with that saying, but I know a long walk in the rain is always calming to me. This drive was perfect. The rain was slowly falling, and the love of my life was sleeping in my back seat.

The rain cleansing me of my sins. [author's note: add a nursery rhyme about the rain?]

Chapter XX

Before we left D'Arcy's place, I had gently placed some ties around her wrists and her feet, and I [author's note: research method to keep D'Arcy asleep since the blow to the head would typically only cause temporary unconsciousness]. I didn't expect her to sleep this long, but I was glad she did. It gave me some time after we got home to tidy up the place. Our first dinner at my place—our place—needed to be perfect. I couldn't have her first impression of our home-to-be that of a messy person. I always kept the house clean. Living alone in a small house, it was easy to do.

D'Arcy was lying on the sofa when she finally woke.

"Good evening my angel," I said. "You've woken up just in time for dinner. I've never made a vegetarian meal before. I hope you like it."

"When I went to the grocery store there were a lot of things that were meatless options, which I found to be odd. Why would I buy a meatless fried chicken when I could just buy a real fried chicken?" I glanced at her laying on the sofa.

"I decided on a block of tofu," I said. "I read how to make it crispy, which I think sounded better. So we are having crispy tofu with stir-fried vegetables."

I removed the tape from her mouth.

"Denton, what are you doing?" D'Arcy asked. "You better untie me now."

CHAPTER EIGHT
JASON SHAW

Leigh Anne was wiping the chocolate sauce from the corner of her mouth. Today we had met for ice cream. It was a warm day, one of the last ones before the unbearable temperatures of the summer started.

"How did he run up the stairs if she just shot him in the leg?" she asked.

"What?" I mumbled. I had a mouthful of mint chocolate chip, the white kind. The green kind is trash.

"How did Denton run up the stairs after he carried her down the stairs with a fresh bullet wound in his leg?" Leigh Anne asked.

"I don't know. I guess I missed that little error," I replied. "Apparently, I drank a lot when I was writing that part."

"Are you ready for this?" she asked.

I knew something big was about to come.

That's what she said.

Whoa.

I knew I thought it, but I had never heard it like that in my head before. It was as if someone else was in my head saying it to me.

Odd.

"I need to be honest; I don't feel any real emotion coming from D'Arcy," she said. "When you and I sit and talk about the book, the characters, and your vision, you make D'Arcy seem like a real badass. You tell me she never takes shit from anyone, yet when you write about her, I don't feel the same passion coming from her."

I nodded. "I understand and agree completely. When I re-read and re-write sections of the book, I can't seem to convey the feelings onto paper that I think in my head. And, don't laugh, but I guess I don't fully understand how women act and think."

Leigh Anne laughed. "I'm a woman, and I can't even convey the feelings women have in everyday life!" she said. "Think of this: D'Arcy is a badass, you know it, I know it, and she knows it. When I think of your vision, I'm thinking Lara Croft, but when I read it, I get Laura Ingalls.

"Just don't get all 'man write woman sexy,'" she said in a perfect cartoon caveman impersonation.

"I know." I smiled and pretended to type. "Paul walked in… he was tall and had brown hair. Stacey was by his side. Her long blonde curls bounced seductively. Her taut breasts peeked shyly out of the top of the low-cut blouse. My mind wondered what it would be like to climb those mountains. Paul stood there. Stacey's smell filled the air as the flecks of periwinkle in her eyes drew me in. Paul sat down. Stacey's lips were plump, like a juicy plum."

We both laughed.

I needed to figure out how to get the emotions I thought and talked about actually written down. The story's whole point was to get the reader to want to keep reading, but Leigh Anne was right. D'Arcy is kind of boring.

She gave me a few more tips. Sometimes the numbers are spelled out, sometimes they are written as a number. The point of view still keeps switching, "Who is telling the story? Denton or the omnipotent observer?" she asked. She didn't wait for me to answer.

"The dialogue is not believable," she said. "People don't say each other's names in real life as often as you are writing that they do."

Today was a beat down and a gut punch, but I knew it was coming from a good place. One time after a fight I had with Benjamin and I was venting to Leigh Anne, she said, "Sometimes you just have to be direct, knowing it might hurt, but at least it's being addressed." That was her being direct.

"This is all free advice I'm giving to you that my editors have, at some point or another, given to me," she said as she hugged me goodbye.

After our visit, I drove to the mall. I needed to do some good ole fashioned people watching. I also needed a pretzel, of course. I wanted to see if I could find inspiration from the people around me. I walked around for a while. I sat for a while. I doodled in my journal for a while.

Adrenaline and painkillers.

I quickly wrote my thought into my journal. That's how Denton ran up the stairs. The adrenaline and painkillers took the focus off of his injury, so he was able to run.

I ate my pretzel and scraped every last drop of that creamy jalapeño cheese from its container. I saw hundreds of people, but it just wasn't the inspiration I needed. I left the mall, got back in my car, and decided to go somewhere I had not been in years.

When my best friend (at the time) turned 21, he had a birthday party at a strip club. That was the first and only time I had ever been to one in my entire life. Tonight, for some reason, I felt I would find inspiration from the dancing girls. And if not inspiration, at least I could get a beer.

I walked into Scout's Honor, Scottsdale's premiere gentleman's club. I made my way to the bar, grabbed myself a beer, and sat at a table in the corner. The place seemed busy for a Wednesday evening, not that I had much to compare it to. There were at least two people at every table, except mine. Five men sat at the bar in the back. There were seats lined up around the stage, with only two of them vacant. There were a lot of women in the audience, too. That shocked me. I don't know why, but it did. The air was light, almost like a Vegas hotel lobby. You know, that mixture of ionized air, a touch of added oxygen, and maybe a hint of vanilla cigar smoke. The stage had three poles, one on each side and one directly in the middle. It was very symmetrical. The lights flashed to the beat of some loud music I didn't recognize.

Two girls were on the stage. From what I could tell, three other girls were walking around the club. I wasn't nervous, but I knew anyone looking in my direction could tell I didn't belong here. I kept telling myself, *"Self, you are here for research. You are here for a beer. You can do this."* Most of the time, I believed what I said in my mind, but not this time. Tonight the voices in my head sounded different... again.

I watched the guys staring at the girls. It reminded me of the one and only time I went hunting with my dad as a child. We were sitting quietly in the woods, waiting for a deer to come by. In the silence, my dad would hear a branch break, and his eyes would sparkle with excitement. A few seconds later, he would hear another rustle of leaves on the ground—this time a little closer—he would smile again. A pure look of primal craziness overcame his face when he could see the deer.

These men in the club reminded me of that—hunters hungry for their prey, waiting for the right moment to pounce.

Eventually, one of the girls came over to me. "Hi honey, how are you?" she asked.

I blurted out in a moment of panic, "I'M GAY!"

She smiled. "That's ok," she said. "Are you here with friends?"

"No, I'm here doing research for a book I'm writing," I loudly said so she could hear. I could tell she wasn't interested at all as to why I was there. She was there because she was working and she wanted to make some money.

"I'm Jami," she said. "How about a dance?"

"No, thank you," I said. "But I appreciate the offer."

I appreciate the offer?

Jami walked away and left me there with my beer. I'm sure she told her co-workers not to waste their time with me because that was the last offer I got that night. I sat in the corner for two more beers. My nerves calmed down after the second one. By the third beer, I was relaxed and felt a little more confident that I didn't stand out so badly. No, I wasn't drunk. I didn't even feel buzzed. It just took me a few songs to warm up to the topless ladies that surrounded me. Is it impolite not to stare at their tits instead of their eyes? "Eyes down here, buddy," I imagined Jami pointing to her nipples and saying to those who made direct eye contact.

I looked at the time on my phone and decided to head home. On my way out, Jami was walking past the bar. I reached into my pocket, pulled out a five, and handed it to her.

"Thanks, honey," she said. "I hope you had a good time. Come see me again sometime."

When I got home, I told Benjamin about the experience. He sat and listened to my story with about an 80% attention rate, which was pretty good for him.

"Sounds like a dirty place to drink a beer, if you ask me," Benjamin said.

"Yep, and I had three!" I said. "I needed to find a place where I could sit and watch women," I continued. "Women in control of their surroundings. In control of their bodies. In control of men. I mean, when you think about it, a stripper is standing on a stage, nearly naked, and holding the attention of 95% of the people in the room. That's a power I don't understand. I want to."

"Drag queens do the same thing," he said flatly.

"True, but most drag queens are still men. Men who are in control," I replied.

"That's one helluva story," he said.

I also would love to understand the thoughts of the men in the club. I wondered if they really thought the girls were into them. I mean, I had been to see male strippers before. I knew they were just there to get some dollars and move on.

Did straight men's brains work the same, or did they think they had a chance at getting with the girls?

I needed to go back.

"Do you think this is like a first date, and I need to wait a certain amount of time to go back before it seems weird, or can I go again tomorrow?" I asked.

Benjamin laughed and shook his head with a smile.

Much like single word replies, that phrase usually means he was done with the conversation because he had the correct answer but knew it was not what I wanted to hear. I took it to indicate it was perfectly acceptable for me to go back tomorrow. In my head, I laughed as well. I was just like Denton. I met a girl who I didn't know and was going back to her place of employment again tomorrow. But I could care less if Jami was there or not. I sort of hoped she wasn't.

I took a shower and climbed into bed. Benjamin was reading an article on how humans were the only mammal that willingly delayed sleep. I knew this fun fact definitely applied to me. I grabbed my notebook and wrote my latest shower thoughts. I was working on a list of ways to not get caught if you did kill someone: wear generic shoes/clothing that is sold at a nationwide retail store. That would help maintain anonymity. I knew that was a good detail and somehow needed to work that into my story.

CHAPTER NINE
JASON SHAW

The next day I came home from a long day at work. Benjamin had dinner waiting, fish tacos. We sat down, enjoyed the meal, and caught each other up on the happenings of the day.

"Chris died today," I said.

"Who?" he asked.

"The Dalmatian at work," I said. "Chris."

"I think people who give common human names to their pets are strange," Benjamin said.

"Well, I've never changed any of their names when they arrived," I said.

We continued our casual nightly catch-up over the rest of dinner. "How's your mom?" and "What days are you off this week?" were always topics. After dinner, we cleaned up the mess. Well, I cleaned up the mess. He cooks, I clean. It's been that way for years, and I'm not the best cook anyway. We discussed my going back to the strip club later that evening. He declined my invitation to join me. He said he had made plans with one of his friends because he didn't want to be home alone. We both freshened up and kissed our goodbyes.

"Have fun at the vagina store!" he yelled as I closed the door to my car.

"Only tits are included with the ticket price," I yelled back. "Vaginas cost extra!"

He blew me a kiss and waved goodbye.

I walked into Scout's Honor, grabbed myself a beer, and headed to the same table as yesterday. It provided me with a good view of the stage and a perfect vantage point to people watch. Scout's Honor had a vast collection of craft beers; I was excited to try them all. I looked around and tried to guess who would be the lucky girl to approach me first tonight.

"Welcome to the stage, Miss Marshmallow Thunder!" the DJ said. I hoped I was in for a treat—pun intended. The music started; it was much slower than the previous song. I quickly learned slower music meant louder music.

If it's too loud, you're too old!

I don't often listen to music, and by not often, I mean almost never. I'm that oddball who would rather go on a road trip with no music on. Benjamin hates that about me. But it means I don't have to drive that often as the driver picked the music, and I always picked silence.

Anyway, out walked Marshmallow, the perfect definition of a full-figured black woman. She stood, at most, five and a half feet tall. I had never been good at guessing how much someone weighed. Come to think about it, I never had a reason to. But I put her at a minimum of 260 pounds. She had on a long tight red dress with two slits in the front—one for each leg. The wig she wore was just as red as the dress. The curls fell midway down her back—which ironically was where her ass started. As she walked, her gladiator shoes peeked out of the slits. Her legs looked like a Christmas ham, all laced up and puffing out between the strings.

This woman was a woman of power. Her confidence was enough to make me want to get up on stage and take off my clothes. Well, maybe not that extreme, but if I had on a button-down, I would unbutton one more! Several of the men in the chairs by the stage decided this was their time to refill their drinks, take a bathroom break, or step outside to smoke. Not me! I stood up and walked myself to one of the now-vacant seats. I reached in my pocket, pulled out some bills, and sat there in amazement. Marshmallow put on a show. I placed a two-dollar bill between my fingers and ever so slightly wiggled it in her direction so she knew I was watching. The music had progressively gotten faster and, ironically, quieter. She noticed the bill and came over.

The two-dollar bill was the most genius scam that happened at the strip club. When you asked for change to tip the girls, they told you they didn't have dollar bills and only gave you two-dollar bills, therefore, forcing you to tip, at minimum, two dollars each time!

Marshmallow smiled and quickly pulled her tear-away dress off before grabbing the bill from my hand. One sudden movement and bam, these two huge boobs fell out of their home that was once the dress around her body. She bent down, took two more bills from my pile of cash, and placed them on the stage.

I wasn't ready for what happened next.

She licked her fingers, rubbed her nipples, and dropped down on top of those bills. And by dropped, I mean full-on high jumped in the air and belly-flopped onto the stage. I actually felt the stage shake! She rolled around for a few moments and then pushed herself back up to her feet. Those two-dollar bills stuck to her like perfectly placed green pasties. She smiled and asked if I wanted a dance. I told her maybe next time.

Her time on stage was over. She grabbed up her fallen bills and headed to the back. I picked up my remaining pile of bills, shoved them in my pocket, and grabbed the half-empty glass of beer. Lesson learned. Never leave a pile of cash sitting on a stripper stage. I settled back at my original table. Moments later, I saw Marshmallow walking towards me.

"You don't look like the typical guy that comes here," she said. "What or who are you hiding from?"

"Is it that obvious?" I asked.

"Sugar, look around," she said. "Even though you're tryin' to look casual with your t-shirt and jeans to fit in, you too well put together to be sitting alone at this Gentleman's Club."

She pronounced "to" like "ta." Leigh Anne would hate that about her.

"I stopped by last night and hoped that tonight I might look more like a regular," I said. "I'm honestly just here for research."

"You a reporter?" Marshmallow asked.

"No," I said, "I'm attempting to write a novel."

She sat down, so she must be interested in me.

My mental voices started mocking me. *She must be interested in you, they snickered.* I've done it. I just entertained the thought that a stripper was interested in me. Damn, she's good!

"The main character in the book is supposed to be an in-control badass," I said. "I wanted to be around women who were in control to get some inspiration."

"Oh sugar, we're not in control here," Marshmallow said. "Those little green pieces of paper, they're in control. Would you like to buy me a drink?"

"Is that code for something?" I asked.

"It's code for I'm thirsty and need a break," she said. "And if you don't buy me a drink, I have to walk around until someone does. Understand, sugar?"

I flagged down the server.

"I'll have another beer. Surprise me," I said. "And whatever she wants." Marshmallow told the cocktail waitress to bring her usual. A few moments later, we sat there with drinks in our hands and talked. We talked a little about this, a small amount about that, and a tiny amount about a few other things during our seven-minute conversation. How did I know it was seven minutes? Marshmallow told me each dancer—not stripper, she emphasized—got seven minutes on stage. Jaydin had just started when she sat down, and Jaydin was finishing as she got up.

"I have to get back to work. I hope to see you here again soon," she said. At that point, I knew it was time for me to go. Neither Benjamin nor Leigh Anne would believe me when I told them about the show I had gotten from Marshmallow Thunder.

CHAPTER TEN
JASON SHAW

I hadn't fully developed a routine for my writing process. Some days I sat outside on the porch in the morning with my coffee and just typed the words as they came to me. Some nights after work, I rushed home and typed a paragraph precisely as I had thought it up during my workday. Other times I sat in bed and stared blankly at the screen on my laptop, hoping for something to appear. Today was one of those days where I forced myself to sit down and be creative. I would not exactly say I had writer's block, but I started to think writing was not as rewarding as I thought it would be. I'm not even halfway done, and there was a feeling of "I have to do this" instead of "I want to do this."

I was still trying to get the emotions and attitude of D'Arcy to come through on my pages. I was hitting that point where this new hobby of mine could potentially get tossed in the small pile of other hobbies that I thought would be fun but just weren't. Maybe I was stuck. Perhaps I just thought I wanted to be a writer. This may be one of those hobbies that I just say, "I tried it and failed." Failure was okay. Hobbies were supposed to be fun.

I always prided myself on being a master of the first time. I had always decided what I wanted to learn, and then I would learn it. I would do everything in my power to master the task, hobby, or goal. Master it the first time.

I started typing to see what happened.

Chapter XX

"Good evening my angel," I said. "You've woken up just in time for dinner. I've never made a vegetarian meal before. I hope you like it.

"When I went to the grocery store there were a lot of things that were meatless options, which I found to be odd. Why would I buy a meatless fried chicken when I could just buy a real fried chicken?"

I glanced at her lying on the sofa. She didn't reply.

"I decided on a block of tofu," I continued. "I read how to make it crispy, which I think sounded better. So we are having crispy tofu with stir-fried vegetables."

"Denton, you stupid little shit," she yelled. "Get over here and untie me NOW. I swear to God I am going to kill you!" D'Arcy was visibly upset as she yelled from the couch into the kitchen.

"I'll untie your hands so you can enjoy dinner," I said. "For now, I need to keep your feet together until I know you are happy here."

I eat my dinner in the living room at least five nights a week. I enjoy eating and watching television. I have trays that fit nicely at my couch, and they create the perfect dining area for me. I brought two trays in tonight. I set them up and put our food on each tray. I had taken a bouquet of roses from the kitchen and placed them on the coffee table to act as a centerpiece to our first official dinner date. Thankfully, we didn't need utensils other than a fork. I don't think I can trust D'Arcy with a knife just yet. I know in time she will grow to love me, and she will grow to love living here.

I wanted to talk so I left the television off tonight. I cut the zip ties off from D'Arcy's wrists.

"I hope you like it," I said. "I also made dessert so save some room.

"Let's pray," I said as I bowed my head. "Dear God, thank you for this day, and thank you for the many blessings you have bestowed on my life. Thank you for sending me D'Arcy. She is my angel, my savior. I know, just like your son, Jesus, whom you sent to earth to die for our sins, you sent D'Arcy to help me redeem my life. And Dear Heavenly Father, please send your light to D'Arcy. Let her know that you, in all your great wisdom that we do not always understand, Father God, let her know that you selected her to be my savior here on earth. She is my Jesus. She is my salvation. Amen."

D'Arcy picked up her plate and threw it across the room. The plate smacked against the wall and shattered into several large pieces. "I'm not eating anything you cook for me," she yelled. "Take me home!"

"You are home."

I sat there, ate my dinner, and tried to make small talk. I wasn't going to give in to her anger and replace her meal. She will eat with me when she is ready. I ate all the tofu. I thought it was good, which was surprising. I admit that I don't think I would want to eat it every day, but if D'Arcy was willing to live here, I am willing to adapt to her dietary needs. After a lot of struggling, I managed to re-tie her wrists. I cleaned up the mess, did the dishes, and sat back down with D'Arcy.

"Why are you doing this to me?" she asked. "You know when I don't open the store tomorrow the police will come looking for me. They know you have been stalking me. I've made reports. They know your name. They know where you live. They know what kind of car you drive. I'm not some stupid little girl, Denton. I knew you were crazy from the moment you walked into my life. I've done everything to protect myself from crazy..."

"STOP CALLING ME CRAZY!" I said loudly.

"Does that bother you, Denton?" she taunted. "Knowing you are crazy and then having someone tell you to your face. Crazy mother fu..." she said.

"STOP CALLING ME CRAZY," I yelled as I jumped out of my chair. My hand uncontrollably hit her. She fell back against the arm of the sofa. She began to laugh.

My mind instantly flashed back to when I was a child. My mother had just walked into my room to wake me for breakfast. She immediately told me to get out of bed and shower before my father walked in. I had wet the bed again. We both knew how angry it made him. My mother always tried to hide it from my father when I had a nighttime accident.

"Only babies wet the bed, are you still a baby Denton?" He would ask me that all throughout my childhood.

As I got older, the bedwetting got worse. "Denton, you are crazy if you think your mother is going to clean that up any longer," my father said. "If you can't stop pissing in the bed you are going to start sleeping in the barn with the animals. At least they are smart enough to know not to piss where they sleep."

That was the first time he had called me crazy. That word would become a part of his daily vocabulary with me. Sleeping in the barn became my father's favorite form of punishment.

I took a thick metal chain, wrapped it around one of D'Arcy's ankles, and fastened it with a padlock. I connected the other end of the chain to the frame of the couch. I knew the first night having her with me would be the hardest one on her. She wasn't talking anymore. She wasn't fighting anymore, but I knew she was planning something. I could see it in her eyes. That calculating look. Planning. Plotting. I locked all the doors and windows to the house, brought her extra pillows and blankets, and set up a bucket with a toilet seat attached so she could use the bathroom as she needed. I left her a glass of water, and I generously fixed her another plate of food and set it on the coffee table. I knew tomorrow was going to be a great day. I was going to spend it with D'Arcy. I was tired and I'm sure she was. I went to my bedroom and fell asleep.

The next morning I woke and went into the living room. She was still sleeping peacefully. I stared at her for the longest time. She was just as beautiful today as she was the first day we met. Her long hair lay in tousles around her neck, her lips parted ever so slightly, and the mole on her lip was there to greet me. She had eaten her meal and obviously attempted to get the chain off of the sofa.

I started the coffee and began making breakfast. We hadn't talked about it, so I wasn't sure if she ate eggs or drank milk. But I was prepared for that. I had gotten a large portabella mushroom and began to sauté it whole. I toasted some English muffins and washed some kale. I placed the kale in the oven to crisp up. After I cooked the mushroom, I assembled the sandwich; bottom muffin, mushroom, crispy kale, and a jalapeño avocado spread on the top muffin. It looked amazing, and I was excited to try it. The smell of breakfast was enough to wake D'Arcy.

"Don't come in here," she yelled. "I have to use the bathroom."

"Good morning my love," I answered from the kitchen. "Just let me know when you are finished. Breakfast looks amazing. I can't wait for you to try it."

I placed the trays as I had done the night before. I untied D'Arcy's hands and we sat there. She looked at the sandwich and finally took a bite.

"This is good," she said. "Thank you for making such a delicious meal for me. You didn't have to do that."

She was right—this sandwich was really good! Maybe I'll write a vegetarian cookbook one day.

D'Arcy seemed pleased with her meal, and she was appreciative. It had only been one night, but I think she was showing signs of liking it here. We didn't speak much more during breakfast. I tried to make small talk to get to know her better and to allow her to get to know me. She was very curious, though, as to where my house was actually located. How close to town were we? How far was my nearest neighbor? All the things a captured person planning her escape needed to know. I didn't want to lie to her, but I didn't want her to create an escape plan in her head.

"D'Arcy, please understand, you will love it here with me," I said. "If you try to escape, you will only end up hurting our chance at true love."

"I'm not trying to escape," D'Arcy said. "I'm just curious about my new home. If I needed to borrow a cup of sugar, would I be able to walk to the neighbor's house or will I need to drive into town?"

"You can't walk anywhere for a while. You can't leave the house."

[author's note: re-write above scene. Also go back and re-write the tossing of D'Arcy's cell phone out the window. I need it for the next scene!!!]

That night as D'Arcy slept, I brought her phone to my living room. I placed her index finger on the sensor and the phone unlocked. There were a few texts from people I didn't know. Most importantly, there was a voicemail from Stevie. Stevie's grandmother had passed away, and she was calling D'Arcy to let her know she would not be into work for the rest of the week. She told D'Arcy she hoped she understood, and she will call her next week.

My mind was at ease. No one would miss her right away. The more time I have alone with her the better. That means I have more time for her to fall in love with me.

I need to send flowers to Stevie.

That was the last thought I remembered having before falling asleep. Being a great boyfriend is exhausting.

Chapter XX

At noon I looked at the clock. I knew Stevie was not entering Flower's Child.

D'Arcy did not.

I knew Stevie was not finding D'Arcy's apartment empty.

D'Arcy did not.

I knew Stevie was not calling the police.

D'Arcy did not.

I knew Stevie was not being the hero D'Arcy wanted.

D'Arcy did not.

The store stayed closed, the apartment stayed empty, and D'Arcy stayed chained to the couch.

"Tell me about your favorite time of year," D'Arcy said.

"Summer," I answered. "Because it's my vacation from work."

"Summer?" D'Arcy let out a small laugh. "Fall is the best. The colors of the trees changing. The weather cools off. I get to layer my clothes and pumpkin spice everything. Just kidding, I hate pumpkin spice everything!"

"I love pumpkin bread," I said. "I make it every year. Pumpkin is delicious! Pumpkin pie, pumpkin muffins, pumpkin candles, and even pumpkin seeds!" I said. "My mother taught me to bake pumpkin bread when I was young. I look forward to it every year now that she has passed. It's my way of spending time with her, even though she is no longer with me."

We sat there and talked. I will admit it wasn't like talking to a best friend, and it wasn't like talking to a girlfriend, but it also wasn't like talking to a stranger. We were going to make a great couple. I could sense she was still anxious, but in time I would be able to keep her hands free all the time.

I turned the television volume up to a sensible level. I asked what show she would like me to put it on while I prepared our lunch. She said she didn't have a preference, so I left it on a daytime soap opera. I left the room and began preparing lunch. I got to use my favorite kitchen tool, the vegetable spiral cutter. Zucchini spiraled, steamed, and blended with a basil pesto sauce and toasted pine nuts for a little extra crunch. I added sautéed mushrooms as well, my favorite. In D'Arcy's portion I had mixed in some Xanax. I needed to keep her safe, and a tired girl is a safe girl. She wouldn't be able to run as fast if she did escape.

"What prompted you to become a vegetarian?" I asked.

"I grew up in a vegetarian home," she said. "It's all I've ever known. I've never eaten meat in my life. I've never worn leather, eaten a marshmallow, or had any down pillows."

"That sounds like vegan, not vegetarian," I said.

"I love buttered popcorn, milk and cookies, and brownies too much. I couldn't go all the way vegan," she said.

I nodded.

"Denton, could you unchain my legs?" D'Arcy asked. "I won't run. I'm enjoying our time."

I sat there, contemplating the options. I knew the chances of her getting away were not very good, but I'm not sure what she would do to me physically. She could pick up the lamp, hit me over the head, knock me out, steal the keys to the car, and drive away. But, I had left her hands untied since she woke this morning, so I guess she has had that chance already.

She could pull an arrow from my grandpa's quiver I keep in the corner and stab me. My grandpa taught me to shoot a bow and arrow at a young age; I was good at target practice. I know she's studied the room, she knows they are there.

"Tomorrow," I said.

I got up and went to the kitchen to refill our waters. I placed the water on the tray for D'Arcy and went to my bedroom. I wanted to avoid any more talk of removing the chain.

"Denton!" D'Arcy yelled.

I rubbed my eyes to help revive me from my unexpected nap. I looked at my alarm clock, it was 7:03 p.m.

"DENTON!" She yelled again. "You sick fuck! If you drug me again I will kill you."

I heard so much racket from the living room. I wanted to avoid it. I stayed in my room for another hour.

"Have you calmed down?" I asked.

"What time is it?" she asked.

"It's 8."

I could tell she was thinking about why she wasn't rescued yet. Her concern was clearly showing.

I wasn't feeling like cooking dinner for either of us this late. She will have to just eat what I give her. I put a frozen cheese pizza in the oven. When the timer went off, I retrieved the pizza from the hot oven; I placed in on the cutting board and cut it in neat triangles.

Three sides.

Odd.

We ate together; however, there was not much small talk. It was silent other than the crunch of the crispy crust. After we ate, I cleaned the dishes and told my love goodnight.

I went to my bedroom and pulled out my journal. I have kept a journal since I was 5. I still have every one of them. I pulled out my current one, and a magazine article fell to the floor.

"Targeted Individuals: How to Survive and How to Fight Back"

I re-read the article about a group of people who feel the government has targeted them. According to the article, these people believe they are part of a top-secret government experiment. They feel cameras have been watching them, people have followed them, their friends and family have been paid to pretend the 'targeted individuals' are going crazy. Eventually, the government uses the technology to control the individual's mind.

I was one of those people.

[author's note: change the following to the same font that was used in Denton's last note to D'Arcy. Maybe look up some more 'technology' that could be used to control the individual's minds.]

Jan 24. I know they are still trying to implant me with a tracking device. Today after lunch I went to the restroom that all the students use. Usually I use the faculty restroom, but something told me not to today. I pushed the button to get the soap and began to scrub my hands. Instantly it felt like small devices were being pushed into my skin. I know they put something in the soap, some small tracking device that would enter my hands as I was rubbing the soap around. I rinsed the soap off and flung my hands to dry them. I was afraid to use paper towels because what if that would help to push the trackers in.

Jan 26. Peter, Peter pumpkin eater had a wife and couldn't keep her he put her in a pumpkin shell and there he kept her very well

I flipped and read a few more pages.

February 16. Driving home from class there was a tracker following me. They followed me for three miles before they turned. I slowed down to five miles under the speed limit to let them pass, but they didn't. I finally pulled off to the side of the road to pretend to check a text and they drove by.

February 18. I am going to throw away my computer today. I need to get myself disconnected from all of the technology. I don't know where they have hidden the cameras in my house, but I always hear the hum coming from the walls from the power sources of their cameras, speakers, and microphones.

February 19. Matthew 27:42. He saved others, himself he cannot save

The more I read the more I noticed an unusual thing. My handwriting was becoming messy. Almost to the point of not being able to read it at all.

[author's note: calculate the date of this journal entry based on the timeline of when Denton sees the magazine for the first time]

[date]

Dearest Heavenly Father, I come here before you to ask for your forgiveness and your blessings. I hear you speaking to me every day, and now I am here to answer your call. Yesterday you told me my wife would find me soon. Today I found her. I know I have failed you in the past, but I am here today to allow you to guide me. Father God, please tell me how to fulfill your work in getting this lady to be my other half.

Written over the top of the above entry in a red flare marker were the words, 'when i talk to god, people tell me i'm praying. when god talks to me people tell me i must be crazy' [author's note, don't capitalize god or I in the final draft]

CHAPTER ELEVEN
JASON SHAW

"I love your little author's notes throughout the book," Leigh Anne said. "They continue to make me smile. This is one helluva story you are writing."

"Thanks," I replied. "I've added them as I write and don't have the time or energy to look something up. Sometimes I add them after you and I have our dates as a reminder of your feedback, and one more time, thank you for my notebook!

"I still haven't solved the point of view issue I keep having. I think it might be fun to write the book from both of their point of views." I paused. "Points of view? You know, Denton tells his perspective, and then the very next chapter is just a retelling of the same chapter from D'Arcy's point of view."

Leigh Anne nodded.

"But I don't know yet. I'm just writing now to get it all out of my head, and then I'll go back and fix those things," I said.

"You are on no deadline, my friend. I say try different things," she said. "You never know what you will end up liking. Side note: you don't always have to take the reader with you when you fall down your research rabbit holes. The targeted individuals section seems out of place. It doesn't add to the story."

"I know, that's a problem I know I have. I just read something and feel it needs to be shared with the world! Have you ever read about targeted individuals?"

She shook her head.

"But the real question is, what am I going to do for the next three weeks?" I asked.

Leigh Anne sat there and laughed. "I'm coming back. Three weeks will fly by. Just think of the things we will have to talk about when I get back."

"But what if Tiffani, with two *i*'s, two hearts, not dots, starves because you aren't there to cook her favorite non-fat vanilla latke, or whatever it is you cook for her," I said. I always laughed when I thought of the first time Leigh Anne told me the story of when she met Tiffani. The voice Leigh Anne uses when telling me about the "two i's must be dotted with hearts when anyone writes her name" always cheers up any bad situation.

Leigh Anne was leaving tomorrow to head to Hawaii for three weeks. She was going to do research for the book she is currently working on, *In the Shadow of the Rain*. I'm proud to say that I came up with the title for her.

She was hoping to research island life on Niihau, the Forbidden Island. I had to research this little island for myself when she first told me about it. Summary: a rich lady bought the island from the Kingdom of Hawaii a long time ago. The island is off-limits to anyone who is not a descendant of the aforementioned rich lady. There are no roads or running water and the village's only source of electricity is solar-generated. The people speak Hawaiian. Leigh Anne doesn't. She had somehow booked a private safari trip to get herself on the island, and somehow she plans to sneak away from her guide to interview the remaining natives living on the island. Again, Leigh Anne doesn't speak Hawaiian. I think she's just booked herself for a trip to the local jail, which in my mind is a hut made of straw, but I'm sure I'm 100% wrong on that fact. Give me a break! When I go on vacation and tell people I'm from Arizona, they still ask if everyone rides a horse to work. Thanks, John Wayne.

"What do you want me to bring you back from Hawaii?" she asked.

"A ukulele," I said. "Or is it an ukulele?"

"In Hawaii, it's pronounced OO-koo-ley-ley, heavy emphasis on the OO. So you would correctly say an ukulele," she said. "Just what exactly are you going to do with an ukulele?" She overstressed the OO sound and ended it with a wink.

"When did you learn proper Hawaiian speech?" I asked. "I need a new hobby if this whole book thing doesn't pan out!"

"You're doing great. You will finish it when it's time to be finished. It's not a race."

We finished our Sonoran dogs and washed them down with a cold beer.

I hugged Leigh Anne goodbye. It was a good-ole-two-arms-pulled-in-tight hug this time. I told her to send me photos and texts from her work trip. She corrected me the first time when she told me about her trip and I referred to it as a vacation. But to me, Hawaii is a place everyone goes to for a vacation, not for work.

I didn't want to go home to sit and pretend to write, so I decided to head back to Scout's Honor. I did the usual—walked in, grabbed myself a beer, and found my seat in the corner. I had sat there three times now, so I was already calling it my usual seat. Three girls were simultaneously dancing on the stage. The music was loud, and the lights were flashing. Through the crowd and the darkness, I noticed Marshmallow walking around, trying to get someone to take her up on her offers for a dance.

I flagged down the cocktail server and told her I'd like to share a bottle of champagne with Marshmallow. She smiled and said to follow her. I had already researched a champagne dance and felt right at home as I asked for one. I left my chair, and she led me to a room to the right of the stage. I walked in, looked around, and sat down on the red leather sofa that was centered on the wall. The server left me alone. I sat there and examined my surroundings. The smell was horrific: a strange mixture of the vanilla cigar smell in the main room of the club mixed with lemon Lysol, beer, and a faint hint of marijuana. There was a wall that was entirely a mirror and, I might add, completely streak-free. I wish I could get my mirrors that clean. The walls were painted blood red, the ceiling was black, and the floors were a brown tile that was supposed to resemble hardwood. A gold six-bulb chandelier hung from the center of the room. The only place to sit was on the red leather-like sofa. There was a round accent table on each side of the sofa. A small camera was mounted over the door, so I knew I was being watched. This room was not what I was expecting. Dare I use the word "fancy?" Tacky? Yes, but also fancy.

Here's your one chance... don't let me down.

The music was sent into the room through small speakers located in each of the four corners. The song that played was the same as the one in the main room, just a lot quieter. A few minutes later, the cocktail server came in with a bucket of iced champagne. I did not specify what kind, but I knew enough about champagne to know this was not the cheap stuff. The yellow label was wrapped with a white bar towel to keep the name just slightly hidden. She sat the bucket to my right and filled the two glasses. She smiled and told me Marshmallow would be in soon.

The door opened. Marshmallow, thankfully, instantly recognized me.

"Sugar, I didn't expect to see you again, much less see you in the champagne room," she said.

I smiled. She was wearing a tight green vinyl dress. It hugged her hips so tight that I thought one wrong move and the seam would burst. She found the rhythm of the song and began to dance. I don't know what it is about this woman, but I really enjoyed watching her dance. She moved closer. I grabbed a glass and handed it to her. She took a sip of the champagne from the glass and then poured the rest down the valley between her breasts. I couldn't help it, but somewhere from the depths of my belly, laughter erupted.

"I'm so sorry," I said. "It's not you. It's not what you are doing. I just can't sit here and watch this. You know I'm uncomfortable, and I'm sure you are a little uncomfortable, too."

"Sugar, this is my job," she laughed. "I don't care what you're into. I come in, dance, collect my dollars, and move on."

"Can we just sit and talk?" I asked.

"It's your money, we can do anything you want... well," she said, her eyes glanced towards the camera. "Almost anything... but I don't think you want to do that.

"How's the book coming along?" she asked.

"I'm surprised you remember that," I said. "It's coming along. I'm still writing, still researching, and still getting opinions."

"Is a champagne dance part of the story?" she asked.

"No, I was hanging out with a friend," I said. "She went home, and I wasn't ready to go home yet. I decided to come here. When I walked in and saw you, I decided you deserved a little break from working the room. So here we are."

"I didn't catch your name the last time," she said.

"Jason," I answered. "And yours?"

"What if I told you it really is Marshmallow?"

"I would smile and say what a unique name," I said.

She laughed. "For now, it's still Marshmallow."

We sat and talked for what seemed like forever, continually refilling our champagne glasses until we reached the bottom of the bottle. That happened to be about seven glasses—total, not each. I had five, she had one, and her breasts had one. The light in the room went dim for a split second. "That's the five-minute warning light," she said. "I'm supposed to try to get another half hour out of you now."

"I'll have to pass," I said. "I've spent an awful lot just for this little talk. I need to get home anyway. But I want to say thank you for the great conversation. I hope to see you again soon. Maybe outside of work sometime?"

"If I didn't know any better, I'd think you're trying to pick me up," she said.

"Marshmallow, the only thing I know about picking up women is that you lift with your legs and not with your back!"

She laughed and told me good night.

CHAPTER TWELVE
SHE LOVES ME NOT

[author's note: trying out 3rd person perspective. Leigh Anne hated this chapter. It needs a lot of editing. I'm just not up for fixing it right now.]

Chapter XX

Denton woke the next morning to find D'Arcy still asleep on the couch. His eyes quickly scanned the room. Something was off. The couch was a few inches from its usual spot. The indentation in the green shag carpet from where the couch has sat for the past eleven years was no longer under the legs of the chesterfield. Was she trying to escape in the middle of the night?

He went into the kitchen and started a pot of coffee. Even though he was angry, he wanted the smell of coffee to be the thing that woke D'Arcy. Denton loved the smell of coffee in the morning, coffee and bacon. But with D'Arcy living here now, he could no longer have bacon, it was a sacrifice he was willing to make. Oh God, what about Pork Chop? He knew cats could survive a few days without food and water, but how long has it been? He's going to have to somehow let someone know to check on her cat, but how?

He filled two cups, a little sugar and cream with just a splash of Bailey's to give it that needed flavor in his. He left D'Arcy's black. He placed them on a silver tray that was passed down from his great-great-grandmother. It was real silver. Heavy. Shiny. He sat a rose in a vase in the center of the tray and placed a blueberry muffin next to each cup. He walked into the living room and suddenly he was on the ground.

D'Arcy kept her eyes closed as she heard Denton enter the room this morning. She didn't want him to know she had been awake all night planning her next move. When she could smell the coffee, she knew it was time. She was ready to make her escape. As Denton entered the living room she had moved the couch as close to the doorway as she needed to get a clear hit. She had taken one of his books from the bookshelf and hit him as hard as she possibly could. The blow to his face was hard and a direct hit to his nose. Immediately blood began to flow from his nostrils. He had dropped the tray and had fallen to his knees. D'Arcy continued to hit him with the book until Denton started to fight back.

"Don't do this D'Arcy. I am bigger and I am stronger than you. I don't want to hurt you, but trust me, I WILL." Denton couldn't control his temper. He picked the silver tray up off the ground and hit D'Arcy. She fell to the ground. He climbed on top of her and sat on her waist. He brought the tray over his head and continually beat her. Blood had covered her face to the point that she was almost unrecognizable. D'Arcy was screaming and trying to free herself from his weight, but she was unsuccessful. Denton took the chain connecting her leg to the leg of the couch, wrapped it around her neck, and quickly began to tighten it.

D'Arcy struggled for a few seconds and then went limp. Her hands were no longer grabbing at the chain trying to free the grip, no noise was coming from her throat asking for him to stop, and no more air was filling her lungs. He had killed her.

"What have I done? This is bad, real bad. I need to clean this up," he said aloud. Blood was splattered everywhere. It was on him, on the walls, and slowly seeping into the carpet.

"How will I ever get this cleaned up?"

He got up, went into the kitchen, and washed his hands. Then he did what he always did when he had a large task ahead of him—he made a list.

[author's note: use handwriting font for the list below]

1. Wrap the body in a bag and move it outside to keep any more blood from getting into the carpet
2. Move the furniture from the room
3. Wipe down the walls
4. Remove the stain from the carpet
5. Replace the furniture
6. Bury the shopkeeper

Bury the shopkeeper. That's all she really was. A shop keeper. She never loved me. She never took the time to get to know me. I knew everything about her. From the color of her eyes, blue, to the date of her birth, April 29, and now the date of her death, May 31. I guess you never really think about it, but every year when you pass your birthday you have a celebration, but have you ever thought that every year you also pass your death day you just haven't chosen to celebrate it yet. Today, May 31 is the shopkeeper's Death Day. 5/31.

Odd.

I have too many things to get done now before a celebration can happen.

[author's note: verify eye color and see if you have given her a birthdate anywhere else and see if death date lines up with timeline]

CHAPTER THIRTEEN
JASON SHAW

"Why is your alarm going off this early?" I asked Benjamin.

"I told you," he said. "I have a lot of things to get done this morning for work."

He never took any time off. It was always work, work, work. But I learned a long time ago to stop saying anything. When I brought it up, he always went into dad mode and lectured me about how we needed to have five million dollars saved before we could even think about retiring. He reminded me we have to have our retirement home bought and paid for by the time we are 62. And don't forget, if we bought the land today and planted fruit trees on it now, they will be mature before retirement as well.

Little did he know my book was our retirement fund.

I hoped.

Now that I think about it, Leigh Anne wasn't rich, and she's written a lot.

Well, shit! Why had I never thought about that before? Leigh Anne wasn't rich. She wasn't famous. I mean, hell, when we were out in public, adoring fans weren't rushing up to ask for selfies with her. They weren't putting our photos on the cover of the *National Enquirer* asking, "Who is the handsome mystery man having lunch with Leigh Anne Auer? Turn to page 15 to find out."

I regained control of my wandering thoughts.

"OK, I'll let you work," I said. "I'm going back to sleep."

But I couldn't fall back asleep. I just laid in bed and listened to the birds outside my window. I had never been a morning person. In fact, it was usually best to avoid me for about an hour after I woke up to prevent any unintentional words of anger from coming out of my mouth. Eventually, I smelled the coffee and heard noises coming from the kitchen. To me, noises from the kitchen were a much better sound than the birds outside. Food is always a great way to get me out of bed.

"Knock, knock," he said, carrying a tray of food.

Breakfast in bed was not something that happened in our home often. Oh shit. Did I miss our anniversary?

"This morning, we are having a portabello mushroom breakfast sandwich, with crispy kale and a jalapeño avocado spread on a toasted English muffin," he said. He placed a tray in my lap, complete with a single red rose lying between the two sandwiches.

"Breakfast is served."

"Where did you come up with this crazy combination?" I asked.

"It's from your book. You wrote it," he said. "Or you stole it. Only you know the truth."

"When did you read the book?" I asked. He always said once it's finished he would read it, but I know unless it became a movie, he would never "read" it. And yes, I know, watching a movie based on a book is not the same. To Benjamin, it was. One time we were on a road trip, I was driving, and instead of silence, I picked an audiobook for us to listen to. I chose *The Shining*. It was a go-to favorite of mine. And since I was the driver, he was forced to listen. The entire time he talked about this not happening in the movie and that not happening in the movie—as if the book was ruining the movie for him.

Shame, I know.

I wondered who would get cast to play Denton and D'Arcy?

Benjamin's voice brought me back from my daydream. "I haven't read it," he said. "I've just been working so much that I thought I would do something special for you. You are always looking up and saving recipes for things you are never going to cook, so I did a word search on your laptop for breakfast, and it led me directly to the paragraph in your story. I wanted to do something fun and cute to start our weekend off on the right foot. I'm taking this whole weekend off. I've rented us a little cabin up north. I've packed our bags. We will leave once you are up and ready."

"What? Really?" I asked. "I thought you had to work?"

"Secrets and lies," he said. "So, eat up buttercup. We've got a weekend of relaxing in store for us. My sister will be here in an hour." His sister always stayed at our house when we did get a chance for a getaway. She took care of the animals and watered our plants for a small fee of $25 a day.

I really did have the best husband. We had our differences, but what couple didn't? The breakfast was delicious. We finished eating. I quickly showered and got ready for the road trip. A weekend getaway was just what we needed!

Breakfast was what brought the two of us together. Benjamin and I met in college over breakfast one morning. He was going to school for nursing, and I was going to school to be a mortician. It was at a small community college on the newly developing edge of town. The best thing about this school was the cafeteria. The best cafeteria cook only worked on Tuesday, Wednesday, and Thursday. So, Tuesday, Wednesday, and Thursday were the days I would always go get breakfast before class. He cooked as if the cafeteria had three Michelin stars. He was very loud and animated, and you could tell he loved his job.

"Jason! Good morning," yelled the cook as I entered the room. Or is it chef? I guess I don't know the real difference. I'll ask Leigh Anne what makes her a chef and not a cook. Anyway, if he knew your name, he always personalized your greeting. Sadly, he knew my name and I didn't know his. I had been coming here so long that I was past the point of being able to ask him now.

The personalized greeting made me feel good most of the time, but I got a little embarrassed that day. I had gotten in line behind some hunk of a guy, and I didn't think being a regular at the school cafeteria would get me any bonus points on the "dateability" scale.

The cook looked right at me to tell me about a new recipe for the breakfast burritos he made this morning. The guy in front of me, whom I would eventually call my husband, seemed annoyed that the cook ignored him to talk to me.

"It's so big, you'll need two hands," said the chef.

And then it happened.

"That's what she said," mumbled the guy in front of me. I burst out laughing and instantly knew I wanted to marry that man.

Our weekend away was just what the two of us needed. Benjamin had rented us a cabin at the base of the red rocks in Sedona. The primary bedroom had a balcony with a view of the giant mountains. I had always called them mountains, but it seemed the locals referred to them as rocks. The best part of this room was the balcony. We sat out there for hours during our weekend. We talked, sat in comfortable silence, and laughed. We held hands, enjoyed local wine, and did all the things that reminded me how much I loved this man.

I, of course, took my laptop and notebook. I was always prepared for the moment inspiration would hit, and I knew he would still be doing some work things this weekend. He's married to me but has an open affair with his job.

On the last day, while Benjamin was in the shower, I sat on the balcony enjoying my coffee. I witnessed the circle of life. A bobcat was chasing a bunny just feet from where I sat. Usually, I would root for the bunny to run faster. "Get away, bunny," the old me would have yelled. Oddly, this morning I was cheering for the bobcat.

Get him.

Show him what you are made of.

Smell his fear.

When he finally did catch him, he looked at me. We made eye contact. I wanted what he had. I wanted that feeling.

Our weekend came to an end. It was what we both needed. We were able to have time together to be us again. It had been a long time since we had that time.

CHAPTER FOURTEEN
JASON SHAW

My phone made the three quick bing bing bing noises to let me know a text had arrived. It was from Marshmallow. Yes, even though we were real friends, I still called her Marshmallow. After she finally told me her name was Nicole, it was too late for me to reprogram that into my mind.

Marshmallow: Hey Sugar

Me: What's going on

Marshmallow: Come by the club tonight, I'm off early. We need to talk. No, it's nothing bad, I just miss you.

Me: OK. See you soon. XoXo

Marshmallow knew not to just say, "We need to talk." That's the worst text that can ever be sent. I picked up the phone to call Leigh Anne to see if she wanted to go with me so she and I could catch up after her trip. She didn't answer. I asked Benjamin if he wanted to go, as expected, he said no.

I arrived at the club at 10 p.m. The place was empty. And when I say empty, I mean literally the only people in there were employees and myself. The lights were brighter, and the music was much quieter than any other time I had been here. I walked to the bar, and Tenille handed me a beer without waiting for me to order. Yes, I had become a regular. The bartenders and I were on a first-name basis. They all knew what I liked to drink. The girls surrounded me when they saw me in the audience, and by this point, it wasn't awkward at all.

They also laughed that I called it an audience. When I asked them what they called the audience, Carley told me "baby birds."

"The baby birds are loud tonight," she had said.

"What?" I asked.

"Have you ever seen a nest of baby birds? Loud, chirping, with their mouths open, waiting for mama to come," she said.

"Yes," I said.

She grabbed her tits, shook them, and said, "Mama's here!"

They all laughed at and with me.

Marshmallow came out the door marked "employees only." She was not wearing her crazy makeup. No colorful wig. No flashy clothes. She pulled up a seat and smiled.

"Tell me a secret about being a dancer," I said.

"Tell me a secret about being a writer," she replied.

"Oh, I can tell you all the secrets you want to know about being a caretaker for pets, but I know very little secrets about being a writer."

Marshmallow looked at me and smiled. "OK, look around," she said. "Have you ever noticed that none of the girls wear glitter as part of their makeup? Divorce dust is what we call it."

I had never noticed that before.

"Most of the guys that visit us are married, and most of those married men are working late when they are here." She held up her hands for the air quotes when she said working late. "If Jim comes home from work with glitter on his shirt, Jane will assume he was working late with his secretary. Then Jim'll get in trouble with his wife, and he'll stop coming. If all the Jims in the world go home with glitter on them, all the Marshmallows in the world go home with no money in their purse." She laughed. "That's an insider secret for you."

"That's fascinating!" I said. "OK, let me think."

I sat there and scrolled through my thoughts. "I've looked up a lot of sketchy things on my laptop. If the FBI ever needed to look through my search history, they would be extremely concerned. Leigh Anne told me that the searches on my laptop would just remain research unless I do commit any of the crimes I've searched for. I guess that's kind of a secret... maybe?

"But speaking of glitter, I just read about a pedophile that was actually caught one time because this girl wore her favorite gold glitter shoes to school one day. She was kidnapped, and when the guy was eventually found, the cops found the same glitter in his trunk that was on the little girl's shoes!"

Marshmallow looked at me with quizzical eyes. "Just exactly what have you been searching for?" she asked.

"Oh, aside from ways people who commit crimes get caught, I look up things like how to creatively murder someone," I replied.

"Jason! I thought you told me you were writing a love story," she said. "When do I get to read it?"

I pulled out my phone. "What's your email address? I can send you what I have so far."

She and I sat there for a few more beers talking and having a great time. Before I left, I sent Marshmallow what I had written so far. I was excited to hear her thoughts. Now, there would be two people who have read what I had written and two people who could give me their opinions. I hated to admit it, but I did think Leigh Anne might have been a little biased. Best friends were supposed to lift you up, and that's what she did.

It made me think of all of those contestants on old episodes of *American Idol* that everyone knew couldn't (shouldn't?) sing. But someone, somewhere, told them, "Yes, you are amazing. Go try out. You got this!" My only hope was my friend wasn't doing that to me.

CHAPTER FIFTEEN
JASON SHAW

Work was stressful today. One of the significant drawbacks of owning a pet hospice was the fact that those older pets died. Today one of my favorite dogs, Sissy, died. She'd been with me for about a year. Her previous owner passed away, and no friends or family were able to care for her. I had been friends with the owner's landlord, and they asked if I would take her. Sissy was special. She was a beautiful red boxer. Every morning when I would arrive, she was the first to greet me. Her little bobbed tail would never stop wagging. Even when she slept, that tail wagged. Today, she wasn't there to greet me at the door. When I walked to her kennel, she lay there peacefully, no wag left in her tail. I broke down. I always cried when I lost a pet, but for some reason, this one hit me really hard.

I had the same routine when a pet died. First, I began to refer to them as a guest and no longer as a pet. I informed the staff that a guest would no longer need our care. I gathered the personal belongings of the guest. This included their favorite blanket, their favorite toy, and a photo of their previous family, if one was available. I took an ink impression of their front left paw. I then placed the guest and their belongings into a size-appropriate cardboard box. The staff and I wrote goodbye notes to our guest on that box. We carried the box to the retort, the chamber where we completed the process of cremation. I eventually framed their paw print and hung it in the lobby. I did the same for all the animals, not just the dogs. There were pony prints, bird prints, and even a few tiny hamster prints that hung in the lobby.

My father was upset that I never went into the funeral business after spending all that time and money on the education. At least I could say I was using some of my schooling by owning a nationally licensed pet crematory and cemetery. When I first opened The Golden Bones, the initial year was rough, as it was with many small businesses. After only getting seven pets brought to us for care that first year, I knew I needed to venture out into other avenues of income. It was hard to expect people to pay for me to care for their pets when they were no longer able to. Most people just sent them to a shelter. I thought more people would be interested in my service knowing their pet would be well cared for until their passing. Sadly that wasn't the case for the longest time.

Pet cremation, memorials, and a pet cemetery were all things that I have added to my services over the years. Those were the things that saved my business and made me successful at what I do. We are now the most recognized business for end-of-life care for all pets in the entire state of Arizona.

Today, I tearfully wrote my goodbye to Sissy. I gave her the proper care she deserved. I finished some things around my office and then asked my employees if they were OK if I left them alone for the rest of the day. Ever since my duck food experiment with Leigh Anne, I had been visiting the pond more often. It had become my new favorite thinking spot. The park was empty, the water on the pond was calm, the sun was bright, and the ducks were swimming. My phone vibrated in my pocket.

Leigh Anne: What are you doing?

Me: Sitting at the duck pond, we lost a dog today.

Leigh Anne: Sad. Want me to join you? I'm free and home bored.

Me: Sure

The single-word reply signified I wasn't up for an in-depth text conversation.

Leigh Anne: C you Soon…

I put away my phone.

There was one goose that stood out from the rest of the fowl. I called her Mother Goose. From what I can remember of the childhood stories, she's exactly what I pictured Mother Goose would look like. One of my core memories is from kindergarten. One year my mother dressed as Mother Goose and came to class to read everyone stories. I miss her. All this goose was missing was a little black hat and tiny glasses, like Mom wore. She swam the edges of the pond, in my mind, patrolling for unwanted enemies who try to infiltrate the pond. I've often seen her chasing crows who just want to get a quick drink or scavenge for bread crumbs. I wondered how she ended up living with a family of ducks—was she the ugly duckling who protected those who laughed at her when she was young?

Leigh Anne arrived carrying a can of peas. It was the first time I had seen her since her return from Hawaii. I got up, hugged her, and sat back down. Leigh Anne opened the can of peas, drained off the water, and poured a handful into my open palms. I tossed them one by one into the lake. I waited patiently for each duck to gobble one up before I threw in another. Peas sink fast!

I tried to smile and be happy. "Tell me everything!" I said. "Did you go to jail? Did you finish your research? Did you bring me an ukulele?"

"The odd thing is, I didn't see one ukulele store during my trip," she said. "And sorry I didn't text much while I was there. It honestly was just a very fast-paced trip. Wake up, explore, go to bed. Wake up, explore, go to bed."

"That's OK," I said.

"But to answer your questions: No, no, and no," she said.

"Oh?"

"It's true, ain't nobody getting anywhere on that forbidden island," she laughed. "My private tour that I was so excited for, the one I paid for in advance to ensure I had my spot? Well, let's just say I got a private tour by some crazy man who had 'allegedly' been to the island, taken photos, stole some rocks, sticks, and leaves, and placed them in a shed in his back yard, called it a museum, and then stood in his back yard and pointed to an island off in the distance and said 'there it is.'" She finally took a breath.

It was common for Leigh Anne to forget to breathe when she tells a story about something that "emotions" her. You can swap emotions with any emotion you choose.

I laughed.

"So, needless to say, the trip was not a success in the research department," she said. "But I did make time to get my local favorite, loco moco."

"I'm glad. You always talk about that dish," I said. "I have to add it to my 'Jason's things to try before I kick the bucket list.'"

"I got a lot of great photos, though, so that will help me when I am working on my world-building," she said. "And Tiffani, two *i*'s, hearts, not dots, survived without me as well."

Leigh Anne always helped to make things seem OK. She never judged me or made me feel bad about anything. She never hid her opinion on anything but never said anyone else's opinion was wrong. The majority of our afternoon was spent in silence as I dealt with Sissy's death, and that silence was just what I needed. I realized the duck pond wasn't really silent at all. Those birds were always making some racket! Honks, quacks, splashes, and wing flaps. Silence was impossible at the pond.

"If you wanted to kill someone, do you think you could get away with it?" I asked to break the 10 minutes of silence that had passed.

"No, absolutely not," she said. "Science and technology have come so far that I think I would be caught within hours. I recently saw a show about an unsolved murder that was solved because the guy sent his DNA to an ancestry site. I guess one of the terms and conditions of the site was your DNA is not only used to help you find relatives and ancestry history, it was also added to a public database. This guy's spit sample linked him to a murder from 11 years ago."

"Woah. Really?" I asked. "Well, I'm screwed if I ever do anything wrong. My prints are on file from school, and I got my ancestry profile as a gift a few years ago. Why do you think there are so many unsolved murders then?"

"I've never looked into that, so I don't have any answer." She knew me and knew I wouldn't bring it up if I didn't have some fun fact I was ready to toss her way. "How many would you say are unsolved?" she asked.

"Last year, 40% of them," I said. "That's 6,012, according to the FBI. I did some research on it last night. And the year before that, 38% of them went unsolved. So yes, as you said, there are advances, but it seems that the numbers are not getting better. By the end of this year, it could potentially be up to 50% of them not being solved."

"Researching the book, and not just for fun, I assume? I may have to start agreeing with Ben on the fact that you are looking up some crazy things," she said.

"Of course," I said. "I'm still working out the details. I think I have everything mapped out. But I still haven't decided how the book will end... will he get away with it, or will he get caught?"

"Do you think your research and your writing is what caused you so much stress today?" she asked. "You've lost so many pets at work in the past, but it feels different this time."

"I didn't think about that," I said. "I guess it is possible. Benjamin has said he notices when I write because I don't smile as often. He said my mood changes and my body language is different. Do you ever have things like that happen to you?"

"Yes, that's why I only have one friend, and I am single," Leigh Anne said. "You need to remember this: you started writing as a fun, new hobby. If it's impacting your life in negative ways, you should take a break and decide if it's worth the stress. I would hate to see something bad happen between you and Ben because you were stressed over a book."

"I know, I don't think it's coming to that," I said. "We had a great weekend in Sedona while you were gone. I just might take a little break from the world of D'Arcy and Denton and focus on the Leigh Anne, Benjamin, and Marshmallow world."

I don't think she saw that I noticed her little eye roll when I said Marshmallow's name.

The drive home from the duck pond wasn't long enough. I wanted the afternoon to myself, then Leigh Anne had to show up. Now I had to spend the rest of the evening at home.

"I have to go out-of-town this weekend for work," Benjamin said.

"That's fine," I said. I tossed my keys on the counter.

"I hung up that key rack thing you wanted," Benjamin said. "It's by the door."

"I'll use it tomorrow," I said.

"What's going on?"

"I'm just in a bad mood. I don't know why," I said. "Nothing you did, nothing anyone did, I just don't really want to talk."

"OK. Well, dinner will be ready in about an hour. Go take a bath," Benjamin said.

I guess you smell bad.

He was so annoying sometimes, most of the time recently. There are sometimes in the middle of the night, I feel compelled to test out some of the murder techniques I had learned recently.

Stop that.

Fine.

Even the internal conversations I had been having with myself were getting mean. Why was I treating myself like shit too?

Bath.

Dinner.

Sleep.

Better Tomorrow, I hope.

CHAPTER SIXTEEN
JASON SHAW

I had been hanging out with Marshmallow for a while now. I always seemed to end up meeting her at the club. I had finally realized and came to terms with what our friendship was. We were what I liked to call 'bar friends.' Bar friends were those who you only saw in a bar-type environment. You knew these friends, liked them and promised to hang out outside of the bar soon. Soon never happened, but you made the same plans the next time you saw them at the bar.

Bar friends were friends, don't get me wrong. They were just a different type of friend. I valued Marshmallow's friendship a lot, even if it was what some would call superficial.

I thought it was time my newest best friend met my oldest best friend. Yes, I decided to call both of them my best friend. They each completed me. Leigh Anne filled my life with the normal. Marshmallow filled my life with the unexpected. With Benjamin out of town this weekend, it was the perfect excuse to get us together.

I made all of the necessary arrangements, and surprisingly they both agreed. Leigh Anne arrived at my house first.

"Look at this spread," she said as she surveyed the buffet I created. I made my famous pasta sauce, breadsticks, cheese sticks, and fried ravioli. "This looks amazing."

"I hope so. It was fast and easy to make," I said. "I didn't want to spend the whole evening cooking."

The doorbell rang.

"It's so good to finally meet you," Marshmallow said as she walked right past me. "It's taken too long."

Leigh Anne smiled awkwardly, but there was a smile. One thing to know about Leigh Anne is don't touch her. She has never been a fan of strangers touching her. Hell, it took me years before I offered to hug her. Even now, most of the time, it's just one of those one-arm-reach-around-strange-bro-hugs.

"Jason tells me you're an author and a personal chef."

"And he tells me you are a stripper," Leigh Anne said.

I shot a look of anger in Leigh Anne's direction.

"….a dancer, I mean." Leigh Anne corrected.

"Shall we head to the kitchen and get us a plate?" I asked, trying to skip right over her comment. Leigh Anne had it in her head that Marshmallow was just some dumb stripper who she, Leigh Anne, shouldn't have to waste her time on getting to know. Leigh Anne "has enough friends" and "doesn't need to waste her time trying to make new ones." Or, that's what she told me the last time I asked her to go to Scouts with me. I'm not sure why she didn't put up a fight about tonight's meeting.

"Smith said to tell you hello," Marshmallow said. "He thinks you're fun."

"Oh, he's a nice guy," I replied.

"Does he have a horrible first name so everyone just calls him by his last one?" Leigh Anne asked.

"No," Marshmallow said, "Smith is his first name. He says that his mother was obsessed with *Sex in the City*, and so she named him after one of the characters. Or at least that's what he tells everyone."

"I never got into the whole *Sex and the City* craze," Leigh Anne said, stressing the word "and" as if to correct Marshmallow. "A bunch of women just sitting around drinking and being better than everyone else doesn't seem like a good way to waste my time."

"It wasn't for everyone," I said.

Leigh Anne moved the conversation forward, "So, do I call you Marshmallow?"

"Yes, for now," she replied. "My job is not just about dancing, but it's also about creating a fantasy for others while keeping myself safe. If people at the club knew my real name, then they could find out my address. Then they could show up at my door like some crazy person and do who knows what to me."

"Couldn't your Uber driver do the same thing?" Leigh Anne asked.

Marshmallow went on to explain about a dancer who used to work with her. "She used her real name once in the champagne room with a baby bird," she said. "The guy kept coming in repeatedly, asking for her, day after day, night after night, week after week."

I looked at Leigh Anne and said, "Baby bird is what they call the men in the audience."

Marshmallow looked at me as if to say, 'I'm not even to the middle of my damn story, so shut up and let me finish.' Leigh Anne also looked at me as if to say, 'I'm sure she's not even to the middle of her damn story, so shut up so I can go home.'

"One time, he told the bouncer at the door in the back that he was her ride home, that she was expecting him to pick her up and take her home," she continued. "He said her real name, so it sounded legit."

"Did the bouncer let him in?" Leigh Anne asked.

"Oh no, Sugar," Marshmallow said. "That's one of the safety measures we have at the club. Every night at the start of our shift, we have to let the bouncers know how we are getting home. If it's Uber, we let him know. If we are driving, we let him know. If a friend is picking us up, we have to let them know our friend's name. He writes it all on a sheet and keeps it by the back door."

"Oh, that's smart," I said.

Marshmallow gave the another 'shut up' look and continued. "The owner makes us do it for two reasons. One is to ensure the girls don't go home and conduct any private business with patrons—if you know what I mean."

Leigh Anne and I both nodded.

"The other is to ensure if any crazy shows up saying they are here to take someone home and they are not the person on the list, the bouncer doesn't let the girl out," she said.

"As in, you are kept there as a hostage by the bouncer until your ride shows up?" I asked.

She shook her head no, furrowed her eyebrows, and started back into the never-ending story.

That's a valid question, Jason.

"Thank you," I replied to the voice in my head.

After taking a bite of her pasta and a sip of her wine, she continued, "That guy did his social media and Google searches and found out where she lived. He showed up one night at her house, well, her friend's house that she was staying at. She has one of those video recording doorbells, so she recognized him and called the cops."

"Wait," I said, "she was staying at a friend's house, and this guy found her address? That doesn't make sense."

"She was spending the summer with her friend, another girl who worked with us," she said. "I guess this guy really knew what he was doing when it came to tracking down women."

"Does this mystery woman have a name?" Leigh Anne asked.

See, Leigh Anne, I told you that you would like her and her stories.

Shh, I'm trying to listen.

The voices were loud tonight.

"Kendra was her stage name," she said. "So, the cops show up, of course the guy is gone by now. Kendra ended up filing a restraining order against this guy because he just wouldn't stop. She ended up moving back home up north to live with her family because she was too scared to be here anymore."

"Did anything happen to the guy?" Leigh Anne asked.

Marshmallow shrugged.

"That's so scary," I said. "Do you ever talk to her?"

"Oh, hell no!" Marshmallow said. "I'm glad that bitch left. We didn't like each other at all. She was racist. Seemed like every damn week we were meeting with the manager.

She even slapped one of the patrons because he was black, though she would never admit it. She stole my money three different times. Three times!" she said as she waved three fingers in Leigh Anne's face. "And the bitch keyed my car one night after I accused her."

Marshmallow just shook her head. "I'm glad she left. Karma's a bitch, and so is Kendra," she said.

She looked at Leigh Anne, "So anyway, long story short, call me Marshmallow."

"The most excitement I ever had at work is when Tiffani choked on a Jerusalem artichoke," Leigh Anne said. "Being a dancer sounds so dangerous."

"Wait," I said to Leigh Anne. "You never told me that story."

Marshmallow gave Leigh Anne a side-eyed look. "Here's the worst thing she ever said to me," she said as we purposefully avoided any eye contact with Leigh Anne. "One night, she was complaining about how I always got more tips than she did. She said people felt sorry for me because I was fat and black. She told me people were paying as retribution for owning slaves."

"'Reparations,'" Leigh Anne said. "The word is 'reparations.'"

Marshmallow ignored the comment. "Kendra looked me dead in the eye and said, 'My great-great-great-grandparents were too poor to own a slave, so I don't owe you or any other nigger a dime.'"

"That's one helluva story," I said. I was shocked. Leigh Anne was shocked, although she would never admit it.

Marshmallow was angered again by the memory of this story. It was definitely time for me to have another drink.

"I think on that happy note, I am going to get out of here," Leigh Anne said. "I have an early morning tomorrow." I looked down. She had eaten her entire plate and finished her glass of wine. She got up, gave me a side-hug, and nodded towards Marshmallow.

"There's cake," I said.

"Oh, I'll save dessert for our next gathering," she said. "It was nice to finally meet you."

Why did I think this would be a good idea? Me and Leigh Anne were good together. Me and Marshmallow were good together. Why shouldn't the three of us be good together?

"Seriously?" I asked as I followed her to the door. "You are leaving this early?"

"Yes, I think it's time to go," she said. "Don't let my early departure ruin the rest of your evening."

"I'll call you later," I said and waved goodbye. I'm not sure if she didn't hear me or just chose to ignore me.

"She's kind of bitchy," Marshmallow said.

"She usually isn't like that at all," I said.

I grabbed another bottle of wine as I headed back to the dining room. I filled up mine and Marshmallow's glass. "Cheers to new friends!"

She laughed, "Sugar, I don't think I made any new friends tonight."

She and I sat and finished our meals. We kept the glasses full until the entire cake was gone. Yes, the entire cake, gone.

"Where did that husband of yours have to go this weekend?"

"Oh, I never ask. He's always hopping around the country," I replied.

"What exactly does he do, again?"

"He started his own nursing agency a few years ago," I replied. "Basically, he is a traveling nurse but also oversees the travel activities of his employees, who are also nurses. Or something like that."

"He just brings home the money, and you smile," she laughed.

"Correct!"

"How about we open one more bottle before I have to go?"

I went back to the kitchen and quickly returned to refill our glasses.

"What about you? Any man in your life?"

"Nope, not in a very long time," she said. "It's nice taking some time to get to know each other."

"I agree."

We emptied the bottle.

"I've been asking everyone," I said. "Now it's time to ask you." My words were slurred. "Could you kill someone and get away with it?"

"What the hell kind of question is that?"

"It's for my book. I just wonder who thinks they can and who thinks they cannot get away with murder."

"I have never wanted to kill anyone enough to really sit down and think about that."

"I have to use the bathroom," I said. "That will give you time to think about the question."

I went into the bathroom and stood at the mirror. Man, I was drunk. When I returned, I had already forgotten about my question. Marshmallow had carried our glasses and placed them in the sink. "I really hoped you two would have been friends."

"False hopes are more dangerous than fears," Marshmallow said.

"What?"

"That's the only thing Kendra ever said that was true," she said. "False hopes are more dangerous than fears."

I nodded my head.

"I called for my Uber while you were gone," she said. "You need to get yourself to bed. Tomorrow will not be fun. Wine hangovers are the worst."

CHAPTER SEVENTEEN
JASON SHAW

My phone rang early the following day. It was Benjamin.

"Good morning, sunshine!" he said.

"Oh babe, it's too early to be that happy."

"Isn't it 1:30 in the afternoon there?"

I glanced at the clock on my phone. "Yes, it's too early to be that happy."

"Sounds like you three had a good time last night."

"It was horrible, babe," I said. "I was so embarrassed. It was like Leigh Anne was just trying to be rude on purpose."

"I'm sure that wasn't the case," he said. "It's just odd introducing a new friend into an already existing friendship. You and Leigh Anne have known each other for, what, 15 years?"

"Well, I think she's being stupid for no reason," I replied.

"I think you deserve to have your feelings a little upset at times, too," he said. "You always think the world is full of sunshine and roses. It's not. Everyone has to have fights, everyone has to be mad, and everyone has to be upset at some point in time. It's the balance of the world."

"Calm down, Dr. Phil," I said.

"Call Leigh Anne and ask her if she wants to go to dinner," Benjamin said. "Sit and talk. Just the two of you."

"I will. I love you."

"I love you too," he said and hung up.

Me: Hey, can we meet for dinner tomorrow.

The ellipsis appeared on my screen as she wrote her reply.

The three dancing dots disappeared.

Silence.

She officially ignored me.

I fell back asleep.

My phone rang later that afternoon, once again waking me from my sleep. It was Leigh Anne.

"Before you say anything," she began, "I just want you to know I'm not mad. I'm not happy, but I'm not mad."

"OK," I said.

"I'm also not jealous. That's the most important thing for you to understand. I. Am. Not. Jealous." Leigh Anne made a purposeful pause between each of those last four words.

One.

Two.

Three.

Four.

Five.

I counted to give her enough time to continue. She didn't, so I spoke. "We've been friends for too many years for me to assume you are jealous of me talking to someone else. Yet it feels like I am the victim. It feels like I am the adulterer who got caught red-handed with a stripper named Marshmallow."

She laughed. "Dancer," she corrected.

"But the thing is," I said. "I really did want you to like her. But you were just rude."

"I was, I know, and I'm sorry for that," she said. "What if I told you my sugar was low?"

"Shut up," I laughed.

"Let's go up north this weekend, just me and you and our laptops," she said. "We can get a nice room, talk, write, and have a few bottles of wine."

"OK, I'll make some calls when I get to work and move a few things around," I said.

"I'll pick you up Friday at 3," she said. "You find the place. I'll send you money for my half."

"Sounds good," I said.

"Have a great day at work. Bye."

"Bye," I said.

I did a quick search and found a little motel on the outskirts of Flagstaff. It reminded me of one of those "oh, we don't have anywhere else to stay out here on this family road trip, so we will pick this seedy little roadside inn and hope the killer doesn't find us" type of places. It had 378 reviews and a 4.6 star rating. That was pretty good, in my opinion.

Thankfully, the week flew by. Friday finally arrived. I packed my bag and waited for Leigh Anne to arrive. The drive up was nice. She was the driver, so she picked the music: 90's alternative. I wonder whatever happened to that genre; you never hear of a new 'alternative' bands these days. It was one of the few genres I knew well and can honestly say I enjoy.

"Nirvana!" I shouted. "They are my favorite."

"Mine too."

We sang—shouted the lyrics at the top of our lungs. I may have altered some words when I couldn't remember them. Doesn't everyone?

"I can never remember that line," I said as we pulled into the parking lot.

"Wow, this is not what I pictured you would pick," Leigh Anne said.

"I assumed this was our writer's retreat that we always say we need to take," I said. "So, I picked the perfect murder hot spot to inspire me."

"So forget me and my inspiration?" she said, a statement and a question rolled up into one.

"You went to Hawaii for your inspiration!" I said. "Isn't your book was almost finished? Like, no joke—you could slap a big fat DONE stamp on it by tomorrow if you wanted to." I had recently started setting time aside that was just for writing. I had gotten so much more done sticking to a schedule. I had also stopped researching stuff. During my research, I found that I was doing nothing other than just avoiding what I set out to do this year, and that was write. Oh, the irony, right? I honestly felt like I could be finished with my first-ish draft by the end of the month. I say first-ish because, as I've gotten advice from Leigh Anne, I would usually go back and edit based on her feedback. So I've probably changed it about 341 times. I didn't make any changes based on Marshmallow's feedback. I think the text, yes, the text, not a phone call, not feedback in person, a text said: That's really good. I'm excited to read the end. So, she didn't give me any feedback. I haven't sent her any more chapters after the most recent rewrite of the murder scene.

I went to the lobby, where a neon NO VACANCY sign illuminated the window. The word NO kept flickering off and on, so I wasn't sure what the sign was trying to say. Judging by the one other car in the parking lot, I could only assume they had not sold all of their rooms for the weekend.

"I'm checking in," I said. "Jason Shaw."

The clerk looked at his computer screen. "Two joining rooms, with queen size beds," he said.

"Yes, that's me," I said.

I signed the form, and he handed me the keys to rooms 12 and 13.

I crossed the parking lot smiling wide. "Your key, my lady," I said as I handed her room 13's key.

"An actual key," she said. "I can't remember the last time I stayed at a hotel that didn't use a plastic key card."

"Look around you, Leigh Anne," I said. "This isn't a hotel. It's a mo-tel, extra emphasis on the mo. It's where killers, whores, and thieves stay."

"Which of the three are we?" Leigh Anne asked.

"The possibilities are endless," I said.

We walked into our respective rooms and opened the door that joined the two. We were quite surprised at the cleanliness and overall appearance of the rooms. They were your standard rooms—a bed, nightstand. In Leigh Anne's lucky number 13 room, she also had a television remote. My room, unlucky 12, was not equipped with such high-tech items. I guessed I would have to get out of bed to flip through the channels.

"At least they are clean," Leigh Anne said.

I checked under my bed (for bodies), I looked in the closet (for monsters), and the drawers (for money tucked in the Bible. People tend to hide it there when no safe is around. I found $37 tucked away in Leviticus in a Santa Fe Holiday Inn once.). I carefully inspected each layer of the bedding. I pulled them back one by one to ensure nothing was between them that shouldn't be. I've found some crazy things between sheets in some of the finest hotels throughout the country, so I always checked!

"I know it's probably not what you were expecting, but the reviews were really good," I said. "Honestly. Everyone says the sunsets from here are the most amazing in all of Arizona."

"I don't know if that's a fair contest since Arizona produces the prettiest sunsets in the world," Leigh Anne said.

She left my room and headed into hers, only to return seconds later with two glasses and a bottle of wine. The wine had a picture of a French bulldog with a huge handlebar mustache. When she pulled the cork, a fruity smell filled the room. She poured the wine. We clanked our glasses and said cheers! The wine was delicious. I was so glad Leigh Anne brought this one.

I attempted to grow a handlebar mustache once; it didn't work out so well! I kept my hair short so I didn't have to wake up extra early and fix it. Let's just say a 'bed head' mustache is not a pretty sight to wake up to. I'm shocked Benjamin never told me to shave it off!

Leigh Anne sat in the armchair and propped her feet up on my bed. She was wearing brightly colored toe socks and wiggled her toes simultaneously to show them off.

"Let's talk so we can kick the elephant in the room out into the wilderness," Leigh Anne said.

"OK. I'll start," I said. "You are my best friend. Hell, I only have two real friends. I value your friendship more than anything. I wanted you to meet Marshmallow with the hopes that you would be her friend as well."

"For the duration of this conversation, can we please just call her Nicole?" Leigh Anne interrupted.

"Fine, you know I wanted to introduce you and Nicole since the first night I met her," I continued. "There is something fun about her that I think is missing from my life. You know I'm not a 'bar' guy, and you know I'm definitely not a strip club kind of guy. But the fun factor that she brought to me is something I needed."

She nodded.

"Benjamin and I have an amazing relationship, as you know," I said. "But we are already an old married couple. The most excitement we have is when one of the dogs runs into the kitchen table during a championship round of Jenga, causing the tower to fall before a victor emerges— and I wouldn't trade that for the world."

"Go on," she said.

"So Marsh-, Nicole comes along and boom, fun!"

"So what? You don't think I'm fun?" Leigh Anne asked.

"Don't get it twisted and start putting words into my mouth. You and I always have fun, but again, like my fun with Benjamin, it's different. You are my everyday fun, he is my husband fun, and she is the wild and crazy fun."

"What does everyday fun mean?" she asked.

"I know you and I can have fun going to a thrift store looking at books. We can have fun walking around doing nothing. We can have fun doing run-of-the-mill everyday things," I said. "And you and I always have, what I consider, some of the most intellectual conversations I ever have," I said.

"I get your point," Leigh Anne said. "But why the huge desire for me and Nicole to be friends? I honestly thought she was very annoying. Maybe not annoying, but damn, she talks a lot." She paused. "And why does she say 'to' like 'ta'?"

"In my head, everyday fun mixed with wild and crazy fun is the perfect marriage," I said. I took a drink of my wine and waited for her response.

"So does that mean if I don't like her, you can't be her friend?" she asked.

"No, it just means now I have to get a day planner so I can manage my huge social life," I laughed. She smiled.

"So here's the deal. Yes, I may have been a little rude. I'm not going to make up an excuse or blame it on something to make it seem less valid. I was rude, and I don't have a reason why. But let's just make this agreement now. The two of you will be friends, and you and I will always be friends. I do not see us ever having a three-way friendship."

"Deal," I said. "I let her read my story. Benjamin is not happy that I am letting people read it."

"And what did she say?"

"Her exact words: 'it's really good.'"

"What else would you expect from your wild and crazy friend?" Leigh Anne asked as she held up her almost empty glass in a cheers motion.

I raised my glass and emptied the remaining wine in one gulp. "Fill 'er up again," I said. "But don't get mad at me like Benjamin did when I let her read the finished book before it's sent off to the publisher."

"Why is Ben mad that you are letting people read it?" she asked.

"You know my husband thinks the world is out to get him. So, he thinks the same about me and my book. He thinks that if I get published, you will ask for some form of royalties because you give me advice and input. Something about how the same thing happened in or with the Facebook movie. But I can't remember what that story was."

We spent the rest of the night sitting with our laptops open, our wine glasses full and then empty and then full again. I left the curtains open to give the room the creepy vibe that one of the passing-thru murderers might be just out of sight in the tree line watching us while he's calculating his next move. You have to admit, there is nothing scarier than being home at night with the curtains open, right? If it were up to me, I would never open the curtains. Sometimes it's safer not knowing what is out there.

"I think I'm going to tell Tiffani that I no longer want to be her personal chef," Leigh Anne said.

"What's brought that decision on?" I asked. "And that reminds me, what's the difference between a cook and a chef?"

"I honestly just miss writing full time," she said. "I starting "cheffing" because I love to cook. Now it's what I do the most. I think I don't want to do that as much. Cooking makes me happy. Writing makes me feel fulfilled."

"I can understand that," I said. "I think writing is stressful. I think it's the hardest hobby I have ever taken on. I honestly thought I would sit down one weekend and bust out a bestseller. It has been what, seven, eight-ish months, and I'm barely to the three-quarter mark."

"It took me almost three years to finish my first one, so I think you are doing quite well," she said. "And I didn't have someone as everyday as me and wild and crazy as Nicole to give me advice."

"You are not gonna let it die, are you?" I asked.

"Nope. Not at all," she said. "As for the difference between a chef and a cook, it all comes down to money. If you are paid, you are a chef. If you are not, then you are a cook."

As our weekend came to an end, I realized the energy and motivation I got from Leigh Anne was just what I needed. I got so much more written this weekend than I thought I could possibly write. Maybe it was the wine. Maybe it was the strip club Leigh Anne made me promise never to tell anyone we went to. Maybe it was the motel. Maybe it was a combination of everything that weekend, but I felt pleased with the progress and was thankful for the much-needed time with my best friend.

CHAPTER EIGHTEEN
CHARLI PLATT

Franki thankfully didn't return to Phoenix after graduation. She got herself an apartment in Flagstaff in the same building I lived in. We were neighbors, with two floors and a few doors separating us. It was what I think we both needed. Close enough to each other when we wanted and far enough away when we needed.

I had gotten an internship at a local paper a few months ago. As an intern, I made barely enough money to pay for the gas to get myself to and from work. I knew dancing would continue to give me the income I needed to survive a few more months with the intern salary. Franki, I think, really just loved dancing. She never started looking for a different job.

Franki came over to help me pack after work. I was heading to Denver to see my old college roommate. Working nights had always kept our schedule a little off. She would usually stay up until 5:00 in the morning. I was just always tired. Late nights, early mornings, afternoon interviews—my schedule was all over the place.

"What's this about?" she asked as she held up a book.

"I grabbed it out of the Little Free Library near work a few days ago. I had never heard of it so I knew I would love it."

"*Böhmwind* by Leigh Anne Auer," she said.

"It's very entertaining. It's about this guy, Tomas, who works with this scientist in the Old West. He travels through time to various locations and times, obviously." We both laughed.

"The odd thing is the machine can only work when out of the ordinary weather happens."

"Uh huh," she said.

"So the scientist made the machine, and a huge haboob happens, but back then, they weren't sure what it really was. Anyway, Tomas is transported to this place called Upper Franconia in the early 1800s."

"So not much of a time travel then?" she asked. "Just a location jump?"

"Well, yes. I guess you could say that," I continued. "But anyway, he meets this lady who is the daughter of a local beer maker. She's sort of a prisoner, I think. It hasn't been explained, yet. But anyway, I'll just say it's kept my attention. I'll give you the full run down when I get back."

"Does he speak, where did you say he was..? Franconian?" Franki laughed at her made-up word.

"Yes, I think. Everyone speaks English. Maybe it's part of the time-traveling ability."

Franki smiled. "Sounds like one helluva story."

CHAPTER NINETEEN
JASON SHAW

"How was your weekend?" Benjamin asked. He greeted me at the door with a kiss.

"It was what we needed," I said. "We talked and got things worked out. I do think it was a tad blown out of proportion."

"And the hotel?"

"Oh babe, it was far from a hotel," I said. "It was a shady little motel in the middle of nowhere."

"Why do you always find yourself in those types of places?" Benjamin asked.

"I like to live on the wild side," I said as I reached my arms around him to give him another kiss.

"You will never guess what else we did," I said.

"What?"

"Leigh Anne took me to a strip club," I said.

"Again, why do you always find yourself in those types of places?" he laughed.

"It was some form of her saying, 'it's not that I don't like strip clubs, it's more of I don't like Marshmallow,'" I said. "Also, I think we saw Kendra there."

"Who?" Benjamin asked.

"The stripper Marshmallow was telling us about," I said. "The one who was racist and mean to her."

"Why do you think you saw her?" Benjamin asked.

"Well, first of all, her name was Kendra," I explained. "Second of all, she had this tattoo on her arm that said

'False Hopes Are More Dangerous Than Fears.'" I then went on to remind him about how Marshmallow told me that quote was the only thing she ever agreed with Kendra about and blah, blah, blah.

"Don't you think if someone were stalking her, she would have changed her stage name?" he asked.

"Well, maybe," I said. "I guess that never really entered my mind until now."

I would have to tell Marshmallow the news when I saw her next.

"And your book? How far did you get?" he asked.

"Really far!" I replied. "I think I'm setting myself a goal to be 100% completed in the next two months."

"Are you still having fun with the writing adventure?" Benjamin asked.

"An adventure is accurate," I said. "I'll say this. It is something that has caused me more stress than I expected. It has been a lot of work. And the mental stress has been as bad as it was during my second year of school." That was also when I first started to notice the voices. I ignored them back then.

"I can tell when you are working on parts of the book that are more stressful," he said. "Your mood changes for about two days. When that happens, I know something awful has just happened in the book."

"It's true," I said. "And I'm sorry if it has made you uncomfortable."

"Oh, I'm not uncomfortable," Benjamin said. "I also don't want you to think that just because I haven't read your book doesn't mean that I am not interested in your story. I enjoy it when you have a good idea and you take the time to sit down and tell me what happened. It honestly does make me smile when you start off a story with, 'You will never guess what Denton did today.'"

That made me smile.

"But I also don't want to read it until it's finished," he continued. "I've only read the few pages with your breakfast recipe, and I felt bad about doing that. I don't want to influence your story. I want this to be yours. But it does upset me that you let Marshmallow and Leigh Anne read it."

"Why? I value their opinions."

"You have every reason to value the opinion of Leigh Anne," he said. "But Marshmallow?"

"The way I see it, the more people who help me along the journey with their ideas and suggestions, the more I can make smaller edits and appeal to a larger audience," I said.

"And the more people who can come after you once the book is published and say, 'Oh, I told you to change that part, so where is my cut of your profits?'" Benjamin said.

"I admire your faith in me that I'm going to have such a profitable book that people will be lining up to sue me for their share," I said. "People are not as evil as you think."

"People are definitely as evil as I think," he said.

We spent the rest of the evening just sitting on the porch, listening to the wildlife, and talking. Tonight's wildlife consisted of birds, bugs, and off in the distance, the distinct call of a squadron of javelinas.

We rarely got to spend free time together, and when it happened, we both enjoyed it. While I always said Phoenix was where I lived, the real answer was I lived in a suburb of Phoenix. Just far enough from the city that I didn't have all the lights and city noise.

Just far enough from the city that no one would hear you scream.

CHAPTER TWENTY
SHE LOVES ME NOT

Chapter XX

[author's note: change to handwriting font to show this is Denton's Journal. Enter correct date]

Date XX

I feel like my life is over. I don't want to eat. I don't want to sleep. I don't want to love. I visit her grave three times a day. On the fourth day I knew her spirt had left her body. I knew she was not my savior. I knew she would not rise. It's raining today. Today I didn't walk in the rain, today I just got wet. I miss my mother. The rain hid my tears.

She loves me, She loves me not

She is free

I am not

Together we loved, together we lived

she left me, and I forgive.

[author's note: normal font]

There was a knock at Denton's door. He sat down his pen, glanced out the window, and opened the door.

"Denton Chamberlin?" asked the lady.

"Yes," Denton said. "How can I help you?"

"Mr. Chamberlin, I am Detective Naomi Parr and this is my partner Tamara Garza," she said. "We have a few questions about D'Arcy Chesterfield. May we come in?"

He stepped aside to allow the two officers to enter his home.

"Follow me," Denton said. He led the officers to the living room. "Can I get you something to drink?"

They shook their heads no.

The three of them sat down. The two officers sat on the couch where D'Arcy once slept, and Denton sat on the chair.

"Mr. Chamberlin, do you know Ms. Chesterfield?" Parr asked.

"Yes, yes I did," he replied.

"Did?" Parr asked. "Do you know where Ms. Chesterfield is?"

"Yes, yes I do," he replied.

"Can you tell us?" Parr asked.

"I'd rather show you," Denton said. "I will grab my coat, if that's okay."

The officers nodded their heads to indicate their agreement.

Denton got off the chair and went to his bedroom. He locked the door. Outside his window the rain continued to fall, tears from the sky.

Tears fell from his eyes.

He knew what he did was wrong. He knew the detectives in the living room knew what he had done. He knew he still wanted to be with D'Arcy. Denton opened his nightstand and found the small handgun his father had left him.

He opened the bedroom window and crawled outside. He walked to D'Arcy's grave. Denton laid on the wet soil, the tears from the sky mingled with the tears from his eyes. His hands shook. His heart pounded. His voice quivered. His world would never be the same. He knew the light that D'Arcy gave him was gone. His light was now the only one left shining. He was afraid he would never find anyone else to compliment his light. What if the only way for D'Arcy's light to shine again was for his to go out?

"She loves me," he said.

The End.

CHAPTER TWENTY-ONE
JASON SHAW
March 31, 2018

I'd done enough research to know how to get away with murder.

I didn't think I could.

I knew I could.

I had filled my leather-bound notebook with common mistakes of murderers and serial killers who had gotten caught. They were the ones I had researched the most. I also filled my notebook with the perfect list of how to get away with murder. Each episode of true crime television provided a play-by-play list of what the killer did wrong and thus provided me a play-by-play list of what I needed to do right.

1. Ensure there was an alibi.
2. Ensure there was a great disguise.
3. Ensure no evidence was left behind.
4. Ensure the body could never be identified.

One: the alibi. I told Benjamin, my husband, I was going to Sedona for a private writing week. He knew how close I was to finishing my debut novel. He was in full agreement that a week alone was all I needed to come home with a fully completed manuscript. I had rented a room at our favorite resort he and I would often visit for quick weekend getaways. I bought tickets to go on a nighttime trail ride to search for UFOs as a reward for myself. That was not out of the ordinary for me to want to go on a UFO hunt as I always told Benjamin about the unidentified flying objects I encountered. After a few days of writing and editing, I would deserve a fun break. I did not plan on joining the tour, but I would check in on social media, saying how much fun I was having. The tour group had scheduled 27 people for that tour. I had done similar group tours before. I know I couldn't identify someone who was in any of those groups, and I was assuming no one would remember if I was there or not. It was also a 'no photos allowed' tour as the flash from the camera caused vision problems in the night, so no one on the tour would have photo evidence that I was never actually there.

Two: the disguise. Over the past three months, I had been preparing. If there was one thing I had never forgotten from one of my favorite books—"killers get caught because they are in a hurry." I purchased everything I needed with cash. I bought a short brown wig and contacts to make my eyes dark brown. I went to Walmart and purchased size 11 shoes, which were two sizes larger than my normal size. I bought ankle weights to ensure any footprints I left in the dirt would be more profound than I would typically make. It had rained yesterday, so I'm thankful I thought of this as I knew there would be tracks left in the mud. The added weight would give me—well, the detectives—the illusion of being a man much larger than I actually was. On a separate shopping trip, I purchased black leather driving gloves. I purchased bolt cutters and a new padlock in the same transaction. It seemed logical to me that if I needed to cut off a lock, I would need to replace it so I would raise no suspicion if anyone ever questioned a cashier.

I needed a large hunting knife for the weapon, one like my dad would use—one with the sharp blade on one side and the blood gutters on the other. Thankfully Walmart sold those, and thankfully my dad's birthday was coming up soon. He would be getting a slightly-used hunting knife to celebrate him turning another year older.

Three: leave no evidence. I purchased latex exam gloves on a different supply run, which I made certain were not the same brand I used at work. The next time I went shopping, I purchased tight thermal underwear, both the bottoms and the long sleeve top. They were skin-tight, which would help prevent any body hair or dead skin from falling in or around the crime scene. I had duct tape to keep all openings in the thermals closed tight. The day I planned the murder to happen, I would go get my hair cut. I always kept my hair short. A one-guard all over was what I always requested. I would carry my newly purchased jacket in with me. While the stylist cut my hair, I would leave the jacket in the waiting area. I would request a quick shampoo because I was meeting a friend for dinner and didn't want loose hairs stuck to my head. After I had my hair cut and shampooed, I would use the restroom and accidentally drop my jacket on the floor. This would cause multiple hairs from multiple people to get on the jacket. This jacket would be worn throughout the process to ensure that if any of my hair was lost at the scene, it would be in a blend of everyone else who got their hair cut that day. Statistically, only five percent of killers were caught using forensics, so the hairs on my jacket might be a little overkill, but you can never be too prepared.

Three months and 29 days ago, I told Benjamin that I would soon be finished with *She Loves Me Not*. Three months and 19 days after that, I typed The End. It wasn't quite the end, but I typed it anyway. I was so excited that six days ago I emailed a copy to both of my best friends, Marshmallow and Leigh Anne, to get their final feedback. I gave them each a deadline to get back to me in eight days. Both of them emailed me their feedback in seven. Marshmallow's feedback was in the form of a shortly worded text message. Leigh Anne's feedback was seven pages long and included a 22-slide PowerPoint! Anyone could guess whose feedback I valued more.

My debut novel had been written, read, re-written, and re-read. I was completely happy with every word that I had puzzle pieced together and every comma that I had thoughtfully typed. I was happy with the character flow. I was happy with the sketch I drew for the cover art. I was happy with my dedication and thank you pages. I was happy with the beginning, the middle, and the end. Hell, I was happy with the end of the beginning and the beginning of the end. However, I was still not happy with the murder scene. It was the only part of the story that I didn't think was believable. Leigh Anne said to leave it as is because the next step, finding an agent, would take up so much time that I needed to start pitching my book as quickly as I could. But like every other aspect of my life, I couldn't say something was finished until I loved it. I couldn't love it fully until I knew it was accurate. No amount of research would give me the real emotions someone felt when they murdered someone. I wanted to see the fear in their eyes. I wanted to feel my heartbeat accelerate. I wanted to smell the air as their soul left their body. I wanted to be the last thing they saw as they begged me to let them live.

I had thought of everything. I had everything I needed.

I, Jason Daniel Shaw, was actually going to kill someone.

PART 2
September 2019

CHAPTER TWENTY-TWO
CHARLI PLATT

"OK, Gwendy, I'll go buy it today," I said. "You know I'm not going to like it. I never like anything that everyone else does. Harry Potter? NO! *A Game of Thrones*? NO! Anything by Gillian Flynn? NO! OK, well, maybe one or two by her. I'm just not into reading what society, social media, Oprah, and Reese tell me is good." I ended the call, picked up my keys, and headed to the bookstore.

I walked into the Tattered Cover around three o'clock. As I expected, front and center was the book everyone and their brother talked about: *She Loves Me Not* by JD Shaw. There were three tables of this "unputdownable book," according to Stephen King. "Brilliantly thought out," per Stan Patrick from the *Washington Post*. "Clear your weekend because you will not want to put it down," advised the *New York Times*. Even the 12-year-olds were huddled around the table flipping through the pages. I picked up a copy and quickly headed to the counter.

"Hey, Charli," said Conner. He was smiling. He had a good smile. The corners of his mouth curved up mischievously. And those eyes. He was the only person I knew who had green eyes, bright emerald green. I always thought they were contacts. "I didn't expect you to pick this one up."

"You know me so well," I said.

"I would like to get to know you better," Conner said. "Coffee sometime?"

I held up the book and ignored the question.

"Gwendy told me it was a-mazing." I sang in a high falsetto, trying to change the subject. "She and I usually have similar likes and dislikes."

"I know," he said. "You both have told me no to a date —multiple times if I recall." His smile became a smirk.

"Oh shut up, Conner," I said. "Ring me up, give me the book, and I'll see you Saturday night at seven. Meet me at my apartment. Don't be late, or I'll never give you this opportunity again."

"What? Really? Thank you, thank you," he said.

"No, silly." I laughed as I walked out the door. Conner was one of the people who always said, 'thank you, thank you,' as if saying it once wasn't enough. My messed-up mind told me it was the reason I couldn't date him. I was just not ready to date anyone. It wouldn't be fair to him, knowing I couldn't put my all into a relationship at the moment.

Gwendy and I had lived together for the past year. She asked me to move to Denver three months after my sister went missing last year. Went missing? No. She invited me to move to Denver three months after my sister was murdered last year. Went missing was what my parents said. They hated to talk about what happened to Franki and rarely used the term "murder." She went missing for two days until they found her body—murdered.

Franki, my twin sister, my best friend, my everything was murdered on April 1, 2018. One year, three months, and 17 days later, her murderer was still out there. Not one of those days had passed that I hadn't thought about her.

139

Sixty-Seven. That's how many days in a row I cried—every single day for two months. I got out of bed only to use the restroom. I showered only when I began to smell. I ate only when forced to do so. Those 67 days were the worst days of my life. Gwendy texted me or called me daily. I responded only to a select few.

"I don't understand why she is still grieving after so long." I heard multiple versions of that statement when I forced myself to go into public. I think those who had never felt grief for as long as I have should be thankful they hadn't had to.

After 67 days of crying, I found the strength to get up, get out of bed. I knew I needed to start to get on with my life. The search for my sister's killer essentially stopped on day 66. The police had no leads, found no suspects, and assumed the person who killed her had no motive. They said it was most likely just a sick individual living out a messed-up fantasy, a case of wrong place, wrong time. My opinion? The person who killed Franki knew her, he studied her moves, and he planned his attack with the precision and of someone who knew what they were going to do. It was absolutely not a random crime.

The police questioned everyone from our neighbor down the street to all the men who were at the club that night. No one knew anything. No one saw anything. No one said anything.

Everyone liked Franki. Actually, everyone liked my whole family. Growing up in a small town, everyone knew everybody. Everyone also always knew the gossip. When little Timmy from East Bumpy Road started walking, everyone knew. When Miss James passed away at the wonderful age of 92, everyone knew. When Aunt Alice's pigs broke out of their pen—yes—everyone knew.

It was hard not to be famous in a small town, but we loved growing up there. Franki and I were America's sweethearts. We were the pretty twins who lived on the farm. The pretty twins who were cheerleaders. The pretty twins who both graduated high school as valedictorians. The pretty twins who volunteered their time to make their community better. The pretty twins who were outcasts because they were the strippers. The pretty twins who brought shame to their father by taking their clothes off for money.

The pretty twins.

That's what we were.

Gwendy came home, saw *She Loves Me Not* on the coffee table, and squeaked with delight. "Oh my god, what do you think so far?" she asked

"I like the cover," I said. "That's all I have read."

"Oh, Charli," she said. "Be open to adventure. Be open to something new. Be open to joining the mass of people who like the same book."

Gwendy and I met our Freshman year in college at Northern Arizona University (go Jacks!). She studied social and behavioral science. I studied journalism. Gwendy wanted to heal the world, and I wanted to be on T.V. We each received a letter the summer before our freshman year that told us about our dorm assignment. Gwendolyn Barrie of Denver, Colorado, and Charlene Platt of Winona, Arizona, were to be sharing living quarters on the campus.

Everyone thought it was strange that Franki and I had requested not to be roommates. We shared a womb and then a room our entire lives. College was the time for us to start our lives apart, but together. I mean, we decided to go to the same school so we could be close, but we hoped to make an impression as Franki Platt and Charli Platt, the sisters, not the twins.

I swung open the dorm room door and saw Gwendolyn sitting on one of the beds. She had a tight curly brown afro that framed her face. Sparkling brown eyes hid behind her thin-rimmed glasses. She had on purple eye shadow and purple lipstick that perfectly matched the small purple bow clipped in her hair. I had never in my life ever seen anyone wearing purple lipstick. She wore a white tee-shirt and denim overalls. She definitely would have stood out in my hometown.

"Hi, I'm Gwendolyn," she said. "I haven't unpacked yet. I wasn't sure if you had a preference on which side of the room you wanted."

"Charli," I said as I held out my hand.

She ignored my hand and pulled me in for a hug.

"Oh, Charli. We are going to be best friends. Best friends don't shake hands," she said. "First things first. Please don't ever call me Winnie, I hate it," she said.

"And please don't call me Charlene," I said. "I hate it!"

She and I spent our entire first day in the dorm talking, unpacking, and decorating our new home. Gwendolyn had an obsession with hedgehogs. Pillows, shams, comforter, her backpack, notebooks, and even her pens were all covered in hedgehogs. My side of the room was simple. I had a fluffy green comforter, a few small pillows, and a stuffed unicorn that my dad had given me that morning when we left our house.

I had driven my sister and me to the dorms. Our house was only about 25 minutes away. Most kids had these huge emotional good-byes with their families when they left for college, but not us. We were literally able to go home every day if we wanted a home-cooked meal, maybe some laundry done, or just a simple hug from our mom.

Gwendy was right, though. We would become best friends.

CHAPTER TWENTY-THREE
CHARLI PLATT

I sat there on the small balcony of our two-bedroom apartment. I propped my feet up and placed an unopened Mt. Dew beside me. So far, *She Loves Me Not* seemed like your everyday-run-of-the-mill stalker book. It was an easy read, but I hadn't found it living up to the hype. Like I told Gwendy, I never liked what everyone else did. I wondered what else JD had written. I'd never heard of him before, but that didn't mean I wouldn't recognize other titles he wrote.

* * *

Denton was becoming aware that D'Arcy knew what she had to do to survive. She needed to play along with the game she thought he was playing. He was not going to let her leave the house anytime soon.

"I think I'm finally starting to like it here," D'Arcy said.

"I'm glad to hear you say that," he replied. "But remember, false hopes are more dangerous than fears."

* * *

I glanced at the tattoo on my right arm. Franki and I had gotten matching tattoos on our 18th birthday. The simple black script read, 'False hopes are more dangerous than fears.'

"Gwendy," I yelled. "Come out here."

"What's up?" she said as she joined me on the balcony.

I handed her the book, ran my finger over the last line I had just read, and then pointed to my arm.

"Oh, that's odd," she said.

"Did I ever tell you the story about my tattoo?" I asked.

"No, it has been there since you and I met," she replied. "I guess I never really paid that much attention to it."

"Franki and I have been avid readers our whole lives," I said. "My mom loves to tell the story of us reading *T'was the Night Before Christmas* on Christmas Eve to our family when we were five. I would read a line, Franki would read a line. My cousin, who was seven, still couldn't read, so my mom would always make a big production at our family gatherings about how smart we were because we could read so well. Anyway, Franki would find a favorite book and recommend it to me, I would tell her what to skip, and sometimes we would have our own book club where we would read the same thing at the same time and share our thoughts along the way."

I paused to open my Mt. Dew. "Anyway, J.R.R. Tolkien has always been both of our favorites. After he died, his son finished up some of his manuscripts, and the book *Children of Hurin* was born," I said. "My, I mean our, tattoo is a quote from the book."

"And you and Franki both liked the book?" asked Gwendy.

"No, that's the funny part!" I laughed. "Franki hated the book. I don't think she even finished reading it."

Gwendy smiled.

"I loved it, though, and when I went to get the tattoo, Franki went as well," I said. "She wanted a tattoo so bad that day and couldn't decide what to get. So she got a matching one."

"It's a nice quote," said Gwendy.

"She wanted hers on her wrist. The tattooist said he would have to stack the words on top of each other, one word per line, to make it look nice. I wanted mine all on one line, so I put mine centered between my wrist and elbow." I traced the words on my arm.

"It's strange, though," I said. "Don't you think an author wouldn't want to use a line from another book in his book? Wouldn't that be plagiarism?"

"You're the journalist, not me! Maybe they didn't know it was someone else's idea. Now, get back to reading," Gwendy smiled and left me to continue reading.

"Do you think the story happens really fast?" I asked before she made it back inside.

"No, I think it's perfect," she said. "It's JD's first book. I found him on Instagram a few months ago. He seems like a fun guy. It was so exciting just watching his feed on the day his book was published. I don't know him, but I am proud of his success."

"Well, that answers that question," I said.

"What question?" she asked.

"I was curious what else he had written," I said.

"It's his first! I can't wait to read what he writes next," Gwendy said as she went back inside.

My eyes scanned the page to find where I had just left off.

* * *

"I'm glad to hear you say that," he replied. "But remember, false hopes are more dangerous than fears."

D'Arcy smiled. "You gave me fear when I first arrived, and now I am giving you hope," she said.

They sat there in silence. Denton removed the restraints around D'Arcy's feet for the day. Denton had been giving her more freedom to roam around the house over the past few days. Freedom to explore her new home. Freedom to become a resident here, not just a visitor. Denton turned on the television to break the silence.

"We return to our top story this evening," said the woman in a blue suit. "Darcy Renee Chesterfield, age 23 from Ridgewood, is still missing. Authorities consider this to be a missing person case." A picture of D'Arcy flashed on the screen. "If you have any information on the whereabouts of Darcy, please contact the local authorities."

Denton turned to look at D'Arcy. "I'm sorry she mispronounced your name," he said.

"And I'm sorry I'm considered a missing person," D'Arcy said. "Let me call the police and tell them I'm OK. I can tell them I am not missing. Let me tell them I want to be here."

"You know I can't let you do that," Denton said.

He stood to turn off the television. "Would you like anything while I am up?"

"No," D'Arcy said.

Denton went into the kitchen to grab himself a glass of water. "I'm such an idiot for turning on the television at this time of night," he said quietly to himself as he looked out the window into the woods. "I knew the news would be on, and I knew it would say something about D'Arcy. She's been here for a little over a week now, and I still don't think I can trust her. Ever since she's been here, I've carried a knife strapped to my ankle just in case. I wish I didn't have to do that. I wish she did love me. I wish she didn't give me hope."

Was he talking to himself or to the demons inside his head?

* * *

"I'm going to grab some things from the store," Gwendy said. "Do you want to go?"

"No," I said. Tears had formed from the thoughts of my sister. "I'm just going to stay here."

"You OK, hon?" Gwendy asked. She came onto the balcony with me again.

"Not really, but I'll be fine," I said. "Sometimes random things pop up, and my tears come back."

"I understand," Gwendy said, "Well, no, I don't understand at all. But I'm here to listen as long as you want."

"It's just scary to think that Denton could be a real person. D'Arcy could be a real missing person, ya know?" I asked. "The book starts out like every true-crime podcast I've ever listened to. It just goes to show you that we live in a scary world."

"And, as you know, from those same podcasts, the killer is always found," Gwendy said.

"Not always," I said. "It's been over a year now, and we still don't know who killed her. That monster is still out there."

Gwendy sat down in the chair next to me. "Technology is always changing," she said. "I have faith that someone will discover something new. Whatever that new thing is will spark an interest to re-open the case."

"It's a small-town murder," I said. "No one cares anymore. You said it yourself; when it happened, you only knew what I told you. Social media was silent. National news didn't talk about it. It was just local news. 'It's going to be hot tomorrow, and a person was found crucified and burned at Camp Hidey-Hole; now here's Bob with the sports.'"

Gwendy laughed. "Camp Hidey-Hole?" she asked.

"Shut up, that's just what came out," I said. A small smile formed on my lips.

"Laughter is always best," Gwendy said. "I know when you talk about it, you get upset. But I also know when you talk about it, you feel better. I will always be here for you.

"Are you sure you don't want to come with me?" she asked as she walked inside.

I shook my head and laughed to myself. She said she would always be here for me, and then the girl left!

I went back to the book that I wasn't enjoying. I decided to skip a few chapters ahead to see if it got better and help speed up the story.

* * *

Denton got up, went into the kitchen, and washed his hands. Then he did what he always did when he had a large task ahead of him; he made a list.

Wrap the body in a bag and move it outside to keep any more blood from getting into the carpet

Move the furniture from the room

Wipe down the walls

Remove the stain from the carpet

Replace the furniture

Bury the shopkeeper

Bury the shopkeeper. That's all she was--a shopkeeper. "She never loved me," he said as he looked at her lifeless body. "She never took the time to get to know me. I knew everything about her. From the color of her eyes, blue, to the date of her birth, April 29, and now the date of her death, May 31."

I guess you never really think about it, but every year you pass your birthday you have a celebration. Have you ever thought that every year you also pass your death day, you just haven't chosen to celebrate it yet? Today, May 31, is the shopkeeper's death day.

5/31.

Odd.

Denton slowly walked to his tool shed and removed a sledgehammer and a lopper. He would have to remember to dispose of these as well. Maybe burn them?

Denton loved his home, and he loved the land his home called a home. Not only did it have a huge wooded area, but near the edge of these woods his grandpa had dug a pond. He always told Denton it was only filled with goldfish so there was no need to ever go fishing in it. Denton had never gone fishing.

Denton drug the shopkeeper to the edge of the woods. Small twigs, leaves, and dirt gathered in her hair on the journey from the house. She was still the most beautiful girl in the world. She was still his light. She would always be his one true love. She was his savior.

She loves me.

Jesus loves me, this I know.

Denton knew the story of the resurrection of Jesus. Is it possible if he replicated the crucifixion that D'Arcy might come back to him? He knew it wasn't possible, in the physical sense, but maybe in the spiritual sense. Maybe D'Arcy's soul would rise and protect him from the rest of the evil in the world. Maybe she would be his savior.

"Is not My word like a fire?" said the Lord.

Denton picked up the sledgehammer and swung with all his might. Her skull shattered.

"And like a hammer that breaks the rock in pieces," Denton said.

Denton carefully sorted through the mess and removed each and every tooth that was once imperfectly aligned in her mouth. He loved that gap between her two front teeth. He placed the teeth in a small cloth bag. He would thoroughly clean them and then use those teeth in the next school year to show his students when they studied the skeletal system in class.

He gently took D'Arcy's hands in his one last time. The blood that covered his hands was now being transferred to hers. There was not a lot of blood. Had it already all drained out? This was definitely not like the movies. In the movies, she would now be lying in an ever-growing dark red puddle. He opened the looper. One by one, as if he were trimming stray branches from a hedge, each finger came off.

"She loves me," he said.

Lop.

"She loves me not."

Lop.

"She loves me."

Lop.

Red wetness formed at the spots where the fingers used to live.

"She loves me not."

Lop.

"She loves me."

Lop.

"It's true. She loves me."

He followed the same sequence with the other hand.

Earlier that day, Denton had formed a cross on the ground from two fallen trees he had found in the woods. He tied the trees together. Denton carefully placed the shopkeeper's body onto the cross. He knew the cross was not strong enough to hold the body, so he would leave them both lying on the ground when the ritual was complete.

Denton took his hammer and five long nails and then began to pray.

"Bless those who mourn," he said as he hammered the first nail through the shopkeeper's right hand. "For those who mourn are left to grieve.

"Bless those who grieve," he said as he hammered the second nail through the shopkeeper's left hand. "For those who grieve are left to live."

He stayed on his knees and crawled to her feet.

"Bless those who live," he said as he hammered the third nail into her right foot. "For those who live are left alone.

"Bless those who are alone," he said as he hammered the fourth nail into her left foot, "For those who are alone are filled with Your love."

Denton stood and took the fifth nail into his hands. He stood with one leg on each side of her waist and gently sat down. He placed the fifth nail on her chest, above her heart. As he hammered the last nail, he said, "And those who are filled with Your love will rise again."

He laid down on her cold body. Christlike. Tears seeped from his eyes.

D'Arcy Renee Chesterfield lay there. The sun was beginning to set. Denton could feel his sins being forgiven. He could feel his pain lessen. The demons in his head were quiet.

* * *

I must have read and reread that chapter four times. Each time was to convince myself I saw it correctly. Each time the words stayed the same. Each time, the words seemed as if I had written them myself. The details on those pages were eerily familiar—no, not familiar. The details were accurate.

I didn't hear Gwendy leave. Maybe she hadn't. Maybe she had already left and returned. I had lost track of time. "I never really told you everything," I said when Gwendy passed near the window. She only heard me mumble, so she came back outside with me.

"What was that?" Gwendy asked.

"I never told you the details about Franki's death," I said. "It's so hard to talk about, so please don't think I was trying to keep any secrets."

"Oh honey, I don't think that," she said.

"It's one of the few things the media didn't report on," I said. "They found Franki's body in a campground about five miles from our house. She was crucified before she was set on fire."

Gwendy's face was blank.

"Her fingers were cut off," I said. My voice started to shake. "And he took a hammer to her face and beat her. He destroyed her face."

Gwendy's hands had made their way to her face to cover her mouth to try to hide her expression. I have seen that expression so many times. The look of shock, disgust, and sadness.

"Oh my God," she whispered.

Tears slowly pooled in the corner of my eyes.

"He nailed her to a cross and then set the cross on fire," I said.

Gwendy gasped, "Oh, God."

"He wanted to make sure Franki was never identified," I said.

"Oh, God!" Gwendy screamed. "You just read that in the book, didn't you?"

"Yes," I replied. I wiped the tears from my eyes. "What Denton did to D'Arcy is the exact same thing that the killer did to Franki."

Gwendy rushed to my chair and threw her arms around me. More tears were now flowing. Sadness, anger, frustration, and fury were embedded in every drop that left my eyes. She held me until they were dry.

"My dad thought it was some form of a display about sin," I said. "Kill and crucify a stripper for all of the world to see. Sinners must repent." I remember my dad saying 'sinners must repent' over and over and over.

"How did they know it was Franki?" Gwendy asked.

A mirthless chuckle came from somewhere inside me. "Well, I guess the killer didn't take into consideration that Franki had a boob job," I said. "The silicone implants have serial numbers on them, in case of a recall or safety issue."

"But the fire," Gwendy said.

I shook my head. "Most of the burns were just superficial. The fire didn't burn much of her body. We can only assume he didn't stick around to watch it burn."

Gwendy nodded.

"They did a reverse lookup of the serial number, and it immediately identified Franki," I said. "But the cops knew she was missing, so when we heard they found a body, we all knew it was her. She had been missing for two days."

"It sounds like JD used Franki as his inspiration," Gwendy said. She picked up her phone, began to type something, and then looked me in the eyes. "JD is from Phoenix. It had to have been news there when it happened," Gwendy said. "That's so wrong." She kept reading. "Listen to this, *She Loves Me Not* is the debut novel written by Jason Daniel Shaw. It was published on September 15, 2019."

"That's pretty recent," I said.

"I don't know much about writing," Gwendy said. "but I can't imagine he could have written about Franki, got his book edited, printed, and published in that amount of time, could he?"

"What if he killed her?" I asked.

"No," Gwendy said. "There's no way that's what happened. Is there?"

I closed my eyes to blink back a tear. "Then why is it the same?" I asked. "And the quote she tells him. It's the exact same words that are tattooed on my arm and on my sister's wrist."

"What if JD is the killer?" Gwendy said.

We just sat there as the thought lingered.

CHAPTER TWENTY-FOUR
JASON SHAW

"Now, I'm jealous," Leigh Anne said.

"Of what?" I asked.

"You! You are leaving me for three weeks," she said.

"Come with me," I said.

"Tiffani would starve," she said.

"I still can't believe you didn't quit," I said.

"The day I was going to do it, I walked in, and she had just finished installing a mural in her dining room," Leigh Anne said. "It said 'Live, Laugh, Love.'"

I laughed.

"I knew if I left her, she would never be able to survive on her own. And if I had quit to focus all my time on my own writing, I wouldn't have been able to give you all of the great advice," she said. "Without that advice, you wouldn't have been successful." Leigh Anne smiled.

"Yes, yes," I said. "I owe my success to you. Are you going to sue me for your royalties like Benjamin said you would?"

"When the time is right!" She laughed.

She Loves Me Not was picked up by a literary agent and published. All of my karmic blessings were released back to me, and the book was a success. Like a real success! I busted my ass on social media during the last months of the editing phase. I was doing everything in my power to gain followers. I made it to 947 before the book was published, which was a massive accomplishment over the 154 followers I started with. I thought about making Denton and D'Arcy their own Instagram pages as a fun way to advertise, but then decided I could barely manage one account, much less three!

I sent some copies to social media book reviewers, who I quickly learned like to call themselves bookstagrammers, in return for honest reviews. A bookstagrammer was an influencer who photographed covers, wrote reviews, and recommended books. The reviews for my book were all great. I felt validated. I felt amazing. As I said before, being told it was a good story from my friends was nothing like being told it was good from a few strangers.

I sent my query letter to two different agents. I never heard from one, but the other replied nine days later asking for a sample. Nine days! I packed up some sample pages and sent them off. The rest is history. While, yes, 328 is usually the average amount of letters sent by unknown authors before you got a response, I had someone watching out for me. My agent was already asking when I would be finished with my next book!

My agent. I liked the sound of that.

Oh, let me run that by my agent.

I'll have to check with my agent before I can confirm that.

Tomorrow I was starting my book tour. I guess I didn't even know that was a real thing. I had seen posts on social media where people had sat in Barnes and Noble and signed books, but I always just viewed it as "Oh, I'm just gonna sit here at the cafe and pretend I'm famous." No joke! I never thought it was something real!

I asked Benjamin if he would come with me and use the tour as a free vacation, but he could not make his schedule work. "You enjoy this! You deserve this," he told me.

So I leave tomorrow, alone, to head out and sit in bookstores and pretend I was famous.

Oh, by the way, I had reached 10,407 followers now.

Maybe I was famous.

CHAPTER TWENTY-FIVE
CHARLI PLATT

Gwendy and I walked to the Tattered Cover. We lived close enough that the walk from our house was only about 15 minutes. It was such a lovely day today, neither of us wanted to spend our day off inside, and a trip to the bookstore was always a fun time for both of us.

"Good afternoon, ladies," Conner said. "It's good to see me today." He laughed. Conner always tried to make people smile. He was a good guy in that aspect.

"Do you ever get anywhere with that cheesy line?" I asked.

"No, but I never get anywhere without it either," he said as he smiled.

Conner was a part-time associate who seemed to work full-time hours. He loved his job so much that he was still working at the bookstore even when he wasn't working. Customers recognized him and asked for his advice when he was on the clock just as often as when he was off the clock. I wouldn't say I had a crush on the guy, but I would say that if I did have a crush on anyone, it would probably be him. Because of that fact and the fact that I am just overly observant, I noticed his new shoes.

"Where does one even go to buy penny loafers anymore?" I asked.

"They are making a comeback," Conner said. "Finding shiny pennies was the hard part!"

The bookstore was busy. Gwendy and I went to the café. She ordered a hot chai with a splash of milk, her go-to drink. I ordered mine, hot chocolate with extra whipped cream.

"G. Wendy," called the barista a few minutes later.

We both laughed. "That's a new one," Gwendy said.

We sat down on the big comfy chairs.

"Do you remember the first time you called me Gwendy?" she asked.

"I do," I laughed. "Freshman year, you somehow talked me into putting my lips into a cup and sucking really hard for a long time. The Kylie challenge, I think it was called. I pulled that cup off, and my lips were huge!"

"And numb," Gwendy added. She puckered her lips as she started to laugh, "Gwendolyn… Gwendolyn!!!! What did you make me do???? GWENDY!!!" she said in her best impression of me.

It felt good to laugh.

"Why did we do such stupid things?" I said.

"Oh, to be young again," Gwendy said.

"Shut up, that was literally only five years ago!" I said.

"What's so funny?" Conner asked as he was heading in our direction.

"We were just laughing at Charli's big lips," Gwendy said.

"Better to kiss you with," Conner said in his best impromptu big, bad wolf voice.

"Stop it," I replied.

163

"Did you ladies see?" Conner asked as he pointed to a flyer on the table. "JD Shaw is coming next week to do a book signing."

My smile faded.

"You should come," Conner continued.

The silence between us was awkward, but each of us knew what the other was thinking.

"Or not," Conner said slowly. "What's up with you today?"

"We will be here," I said.

"So," Conner said as he looked at me, "what did you think of the book?"

"I hated it," I said. "I didn't even bother finishing it."

"Then why would you want to come to his book signing?" Conner asked.

"She thinks JD killed her sister," Gwendy said.

"You have a sister?" Conner asked.

"Had," I said quietly.

"Woah," Conner said. "I'm sorry, I didn't know."

"It's OK," I said. "There are just some strange coincidences between the book and my sister's murder."

"Like what?" Conner asked.

"You know that date you are always asking about?" I asked.

"Yeah," he replied.

"I'd rather talk about it in a more private place," I said. "If you want to come over after you are finished with your shift, we can talk."

"I'd like that," he said. "But only if you want to talk about it."

"It might be nice to have someone else tell me I'm overreacting," I said as I looked at Gwendy.

"I never said you were overreacting," Gwendy said. "I merely stated it seems a little complicated for it to play out in real life the way it played out in your head."

"I'm off at five," Conner said.

"Do you remember how to get to our apartment?" Gwendy asked.

"Yes," he said. "I gotta get back to work." He moved his eyes to gesture towards his boss. She stared at him as if to let him know he was not getting paid to talk to his friends.

Gwendy and I finished our drinks and started our walk back to our apartment.

"It's official," Gwendy said. "Your first date with Conner."

"Shut up," I replied. "It's just going to be the three of us sitting at home talking."

"Oh," she said. "I forgot. I have plans tonight. So I won't be there."

"You are such a liar," I said.

"True," Gwendy said. "But if you want me gone, it's just that easy!"

"Why did you never go on a date with him?" I asked.

"We did," she said. "Once. It wasn't bad, but we didn't have anything in common other than books."

"I understand," I said. "I don't think I want to date at the moment. I don't feel like I am ready to."

"Well, like you said, it'll be just the three of us sitting around talking," she said.

CHAPTER TWENTY-SIX
JASON SHAW

As I had always done, as soon as the plane landed, I turned my phone off airplane mode and let everyone know I had safely arrived in Denver.

Me: Just letting you know I landed safely. I'll call you when I get to my room.

Benjamin: OK, be safe. I love you

Me: I just landed. Just letting you know I arrived safely

Leigh Anne: OK, I can't wait to hear all about it!!!!!!!!

Me: I'm in Denver for a few days

Marshmallow: Oh, nice!

Me: When I get back lets get together

TO GET HER, I automatically thought. When I was a child, my mother taught me to spell "together" that way. "It's really easy when you break it up," she would say. I still think of it as three little words squished together to make one big word. I went to school the very next day and told my best friend the magical secret. I wondered if she still used that trick, too.

To find her.

To get her.

To kill her.

Woah, where did that thought come from?

Marshmallow: OK

The dreaded one-word reply.

I made it from the airport to my hotel. What a long ride that was! I settled into my room, unpacked, and laid on the bed. Yes, unpacked. I was one of those people who always unpacked the suitcase when I got to a hotel. I called Benjamin.

"Hello, handsome," Benjamin said.

"What are you up to?" I asked.

"Oh, just hanging out," he said. "Cooking me some dinner. Going to watch some movies and be lazy today."

"Sounds like an exciting evening," I said. "I just got unpacked. I'm going to roam around and see if I can find me some dinner myself. My driver told me I had to get a burger from a place called the Cherry Cricket. So, I'm going to try it out. I have to be at the bookstore early tomorrow morning."

"You have a driver now?" Benjamin asked with a sarcastic tone. "I just want you to know that I am very proud of you."

"Thank you, babe," I said. "Hearing that means the world. It's just the motivation I need to get myself through tomorrow!"

I was tired. Flying was exhausting no matter the length of the flight, and these flights had been short! I was glad for this trip, as I would be in Denver for two full days. Only one was going to be at the book signing—which is tomorrow. The following day, I had to meet with my agent.

My agent—Spencer Cruz.

I still liked the sound of that.

I felt like what I'd always imagined a rock star would feel like. Life on tour always seemed so glamorous: a new city every night, new adoring fans screaming my name, and the lavish hotel rooms waiting for my roadies to trash.

That was why I was not a rock star. I was an author. No adoring fans screaming at me. Hell, I don't even think the lady who sat next to me on the plane knew who I was. I did fly first class, though. That's the one luxury I had gotten on my tour. Spencer had sent someone to the airport to ensure I made it to the hotel safely. He was, what I considered, my chaperone. On the ride to the hotel, he gave me the rundown of the times and places where I was to be on this leg of the tour. It was the first chaperone I had gotten. I wonder if Spencer didn't like the way things went in Phoenix or Albuquerque.

I could also sympathize with those rock stars who shout "Hello, Denver" to the crowd when they were actually in Phoenix. It was hard keeping my days straight, and there had been missing time. Maybe that's the reason for the chaperone?

CHAPTER TWENTY-SEVEN
CHARLI PLATT

Today was the day JD Shaw would be arriving in Denver. According to the information I got from his Instagram, this was the third stop on his nationwide book tour. The first stop was at Changing Hands bookstore in Phoenix. Two hundred fifty people showed up to meet him. That was an obvious start to his tour since it was his hometown. He left Phoenix and headed to Albuquerque, NM. Bookworks was the second stop, and 225 people stood in line to meet him. And today, he would be arriving at the Tattered Cover to meet and greet more of his new fans. According to his web page, they are expecting an even larger crowd at Tattered Cover.

Today people would be standing in line to tell him how wonderful his book was. They would boost his ego. They would form the foundation of his growing fame that would eventually catapult his writing career to the likes of Anne Rice, or at least I'm sure that's what he hoped. Little did he know I would be in line as well. I would not have my copy of his book. I would not be there to tell him how amazing he is. I would be there asking him why he killed my sister.

After my night with Conner, his outside perspective made me solidify my theory even more. While Conner and Gwendy still thought I was making too many comparisons, Conner could see that many things were the same.

I told Gwendy I wanted to go alone, but she wouldn't allow it. We arrived at the bookstore at 9:00 a.m., one hour before they opened. There were already about 60 people in line ahead of us.

I had been following JD's every move on every social media platform that I could. I was stalking him, I admit it. From everything I had learned about him over the past week, he seemed like a regular guy. He was married, owned his own business, and his photos online showed the life of an everyday man. I didn't see evil in his eyes. I don't see someone who I would ever pick to be a murderer. That's what made him so scary.

Never judge a book by its cover.

The doors opened promptly at 10 a.m. Conner had the honor of unlocking them. He smiled at me through the window when he saw me in line.

"Welcome, everyone. We are now open!" Conner shouted, "If you are here for coffee, it's that way." He pointed to the left side of the book store.

"If you are here to meet JD Shaw, he's that way," he shouted as he pointed to the rear of the store.

"If you are here for love, well, ladies, I'm taking myself off the market," he said with a smile as he glanced my way.

I rolled my eyes as I passed Conner and followed the line of people to the back of the store. We all went up the stairs into a large room. Seats had been placed in a half-circle that focused the audience's attention onto a podium at the center of the room.

A small rectangular table was just off-center. There was a deep purple cloth, the same shade as the book jacket of *She Loves Me Not*, draped down the four sides. About twenty copies of the book were stacked neatly on the table. JD wasn't in the room.

Everyone quickly and methodically found seats. Once everyone filled all the seats, the remaining people stood around the edge of the room. I was sure this event was the largest turnout so far.

"Ladies, gentlemen, and all variations thereupon," Conner said. "Today, we have the pleasure of welcoming JD Shaw to our great city of Denver. This morning, I had the pleasure of his company over a cup of coffee and a blueberry muffin, which happen to be on sale today if you want to pick up one later." The crowd gave a small laugh. Conner began to scan the room. "During that conversation, I learned that *She Loves Me Not* was born from hard work, lots of research, and lots of dedication."

Conner made direct eye contact with me as he repeated, "lots of research." That must mean Conner now believed me. "I know you could sit there and stare at me all day," Conner said. "But I also know that you, for once, are not here to see me. I present to you, Mr. JD Shaw."

Everyone clapped loudly. JD shook Conner's hand walked to the lectern. Conner stepped off to the side and took the seat at the table.

"Thank you all for coming today," he said. "That's a tough act to follow! Let's give Conner a round of applause," he lead the room in brief applause. "Seeing you here today is what makes this entire process worth it. I'm am here because of an accident. I met a girl, a girl who inspired me. She inspired me to do things. Some of those things were good, and some of those things were bad. She inspired me to meet new people. She inspired me to do things I'd never done. She inspired me to love. She inspired me to hate. And she inspired me to kill."

Gwendy instantly grabbed my hand and squeezed so hard.

"That lady's name is Leigh Anne. My best friend. Instead of reading a chapter from the book, if you don't mind, I'd like to read the dedication of this book.

"The beginning was strong. The middle was bad. The end was never in sight. The end of the beginning was cut, and the beginning of the end was burned, but you never let me give up the fight A poet, I am not, let me make that part clear. You're a writer, you said! You must persevere. You encouraged my mistakes and honored my flaws and never made me feel dumb when I misused the word magnetopause." The crowd laughed.

"See," he said as he looked up from the book. "I told you I'm not a poet." He cleared his throat. "And so Leigh Anne, my mentor and friend, this is just the beginning and far from the end. Thank you."

The crowd applauded as JD walked to the book filled table. Conner took JD's previous position at the lectern. "Now, JD is going to set up over here and sign your books. As you can see, there are a lot of you here today. Please have your book ready when you arrive at the table. Due to the crowd's size, JD is unable to take photographs with individuals but said it's OK for you to photo him while he is signing your book.

"To keep the line moving, we are going to ask that you remain seated until we call your row. Once your book has been signed, we kindly ask that you head back downstairs."

A few other employees had arrived to help with the process. They started with those who were standing around the edge of the room. Excitement filled the air. People in line were talking with the friends they came with. Some were on their phones doing what they do to pass the time. Others were reading or re-reading the book they brought to have signed.

"What are you going to say to him?" Gwendy asked.

"I'm going to just come out and ask why he killed my sister," I said.

"If he did it, he's not going to just admit it. 'Oh, I needed a plot line,'" she said.

"I don't expect him to admit it," I replied. "I just need him to know he's not going to get away with it anymore."

The lady behind us kept averting her eyes anytime we glanced her way. You could tell she was eavesdropping, and she seemed very interested in what we had to say. As we were talking, she seemed to be typing on her phone. Perhaps she was, perhaps she wasn't. But she was for sure nosy!

"Look," I said. "He's a lefty, like you."

Gwendy smiled. "Well, I still don't like or trust him. Even if that does make him a little cooler."

I was shocked at how quickly the room had cleared out. The line was moving fast. My row and the row behind me were the only ones that remained in the room. Before I knew it, Gwendy was at the table.

173

"Hi JD, I'm Gwendy. It's nice to meet you." She slid her copy across the table.

"What a unique name," JD said

"Thanks. I got it for my birthday," Gwendy replied in her sarcastic tone.

"Can you spell it for me?" JD asked.

"G-w-e-n-d-y," she said.

JD smiled. "What did you think of the book?"

"Oh, it was OK," Gwendy said as she stepped aside. He handed back the book, "Gwendy, this is just the beginning. XoXo JD" was written on the title page.

"Where did you get the inspiration for the scene where Denton crucifies D'Arcy?" I asked, looking him in the eyes.

"Hi, I didn't catch your name," JD said.

"Where did you get the inspiration for the scene where Denton crucifies D'Arcy?" I repeated. Loudly.

The lady that was once sitting behind me was no longer trying to pretend she wasn't listening. She had also managed to get directly behind me in line. Her phone was still in her hand, and her eyes were on me.

"Oh, that's an exciting question," JD said. "It took me a long time to get that part written. I wrote it and re-wrote many versions of the death scene before I settled on the one that finally made it into the book. Would you believe when I started writing the book it was going to be a love story?

"Why do you ask?" he said.

"Why did you kill my sister?" I yelled.

"What?" he asked.

"FRANKI PLATT. YOU KILLED HER GODDAMMIT, AND I WANT TO KNOW WHY!" I screamed.

My voice was shaky and cracking. Conner rushed to my side. He pulled me into a big hug and walked me out of the room. Conner told me it was best if we left and went home. I didn't want to, but I agreed.

Three hours later, I was trending on social media. The lady behind me had recorded the encounter with her phone. She posted it to her Twitter account. And just like that, I became the person that the internet couldn't get enough of.

"9News just left me a message," I told Gwendy. "They want to interview me about Franki's murder," I said. "Finally, people outside of Arizona will hear her story," I said.

"That's fantastic news!"

CHAPTER TWENTY-EIGHT
JASON SHAW

"JD, what is going on?"

It was my agent on the other end of the phone. "I'm not 100% sure yet. This girl came up and said that I killed her sister. At first, I thought it was some Kathy Bates shit like in *Misery*. You know, someone was really attached to D'Arcy, and they were jokingly upset that she died. But, no. She legit thinks I killed her sister."

"I booked you a plane ticket to get you back home to Phoenix before this really gets out of hand. I'm sure it's just a crazed fan," Spencer said. "The plane leaves in three hours. You need to get your things ready. Better safe than sorry."

"I hope it's just a crazed fan, and thank you."

"You've already got one helluva story to tell," Spencer said.

We ended the call, and I started packing and called Benjamin.

"How was the big event?" he asked.

"Good," I said. "That means you haven't heard."

"Heard what?"

"Babe, this crazy girl started yelling at me during the signing."

"What!?"

"Yes," I said. "It was the strangest thing. She said I killed her sister, and I then wrote about it in my book."

"No way. What was she talking about?"

"I'm not sure yet," I said. "I called Spencer, and he said he's changing my flight to get me home tonight. That's what's worries me. Why is he so concerned that I get home quickly?"

"I'm sure it's nothing. It's probably one of those clauses in the huge contract you signed with him," Benjamin said. "Don't worry about it. Just have a nice flight, and I'll pick you up at the airport."

After a quick pack, a long drive to the airport, and a short flight, I was relieved to be back in Phoenix. Benjamin was at the airport to pick me up, and we headed home.

"Just remember what they always say," he said. "No matter if it's good or bad, any publicity is good publicity."

"Well, I don't think someone accusing me of murder can ever be considered as good publicity," I said.

"I looked it up after we hung up," he said. "It seems the girl's name is Charlene Platt. Her sister was, in fact, murdered in Flagstaff about a year ago."

"There you have it. How would I have killed someone and written about it in less than a year? It's just stupid to think."

"I have to ask, did you do it?"

I was speechless. "I cannot believe you are asking me that."

I didn't answer his question.

The ride home was silent. Benjamin swung by to pick up dinner from our favorite Thai place. We got home, sat down, and turned on the TV to help my mind unwind and help fill the silence.

"…yes, the entire internet has seen it," the news anchor said. "Here is the 30-second clip for anyone who has yet to see it."

The clip of Charli yelling at me appeared on the screen.

"Local author, JD Shaw thought nothing unusual would happen on the third stop of his nationwide book tour. Little did he know, an attendee would accuse him of murder. FoxNews investigative team has uncovered who the mystery woman is and what her accusations could mean for JD Shaw."

I quickly changed turned off the TV and went to the guest room.

CHAPTER TWENTY-NINE
JASON SHAW

"This will pass, I promise," said Leigh Anne.

It had been less than a week since the story had become nationally known. I wouldn't say I like to refer to it as news since there was really nothing to report.

The accusation had done two things for me: one, made my name nationally known, and two, my book's sales had skyrocketed so high that my publisher could not keep up with the demand. I had to cancel the remaining stops on my book tour as Spencer feared it would become a "let's go see the murderer before he goes to jail" event versus an "I'm excited to meet you as an up-and-coming author" event like we had initially anticipated.

Leigh Anne and I sat in the back corner of Triple B's Bar and Grill, picking at the fried pickles that the waitress had just delivered to our table. I really hated pickles. Leigh Anne knew I hated pickles. I was not sure how we ended up with them. Have you ever just thought maybe today would be different? I did. I picked up a fried pickle, dipped it in the orangish sauce, and ate it.

"Well, I know you didn't do it," she said. "That's all that matters."

"No, that's really not all that matters at all," I said. "I'm considered a person of interest in a murder case."

"You have not officially been called a person of interest," she said.

"I got a voicemail from a Detective Harris asking me to call him. That means I'm a person of interest."

We sat there for a while, trying to pretend life was normal. There were a few points and stares from other people at the restaurant.

"Benjamin asked me if I did it," I said.

"What!?" Leigh Anne said. She put down her fried pickle.

"Yep, when I got home from Colorado, he picked me up at the airport. I got into the car, and the first thing he said was, 'Did you do it?'"

Leigh Anne picked up the pickle. "What did you say?"

"Well, the fact that he even thought that I would do something like that really upset me. I spent the night in the guest room. I just couldn't bear to be in the same room with him."

"That's understandable," she said.

I paused to think about what she had just said. What was understandable? The idea that I spent the night in the guest room in my own home or the fact that my husband asked me if I killed someone. I decided to let it pass without question.

"So the next day, we talked it out a little more calmly," I said. "He just told me that the stress of me being gone for the book tour was getting to him. He let me know that once this blew over, he didn't want me to go on a tour again."

"I don't think any of us expected you to become this successful so quickly," Leigh Anne said. "When you got your book deal, I think we were all excited and scared by not knowing what it would be like. So I understand him experiencing some stress."

"I know," I said. "This little hobby of mine messed up many people's lives."

"Nothing is messed up," she said.

"Yes, many things got messed up over the past month."

"When are you going to meet with the detective?" Leigh Anne asked.

"He asked if I would be willing to drive to Flagstaff tomorrow," I said. "I feel if I don't, it's going to look like I have something to hide."

"Do you?"

"Don't you start, too," I said.

We finished our meals. The pickles were still gross.

I headed home. Benjamin was waiting for me at the door.

"We've had several people call, and a few even stopped by today," Benjamin said. "I tried calling you. Everyone is asking to talk to you, Jason. The police came. They had a warrant. They searched the house and took your laptop and your notebooks."

"Fuck!" I shouted. "Why did they take that?"

"I couldn't stop them. Is that bad? Will they find anything in them?" Benjamin asked.

Anger was building on top of the stress that had laid its foundation in my life over the past few weeks.

"I don't know what else to say or how else I can rephrase this, Benjamin. I. Did. Not. Kill. Anyone. To. Write. A. Book." I raised my voice and made a long, deliberate pause between each word.

"There were times you went to a dark place while you were writing and researching. You made several trips up north while you were writing. I've read your book, and I've done some digging around on that murder. There are not a lot of public details about it, but Jason, I swear what I found is almost exactly what happened in your book." Benjamin was doing his best to remain calm.

We rarely fought. That's one thing that had always been unique about our relationship. Fights are normal in all relationships. I think Benjamin and I had about one major fight a year. This was about to become that fight.

"You have known me for twenty-something years. You know I can barely deal when one of the animals at the home dies. How on earth do you think I could kill a human being?" I asked.

"I know your passion," Benjamin said. "I understand that you can and will do anything to succeed."

"You are correct; I would. But I would—I could never kill anyone." I paused. Benjamin stood there for a few minutes, a few long minutes, without saying anything. "If that's it, I guess I'll be heading to bed now."

Benjamin didn't say anything else. He just turned and walked into our bedroom. He closed the door, which was the signal for me to head to the guest room. Again.

I stared at the ceiling. My mind was racing. When I closed my eyes, the past filled my mind.

No one ever knew about my perfectly laid plan, not even Leigh Anne. At this point, I could never tell anyone without actually sealing my fate. I did drive to Sedona that night. I drove around, hoping I would find someone on the corner holding a sign asking for money. People would not easily miss someone who asked for money.

Little did I know, there were no homeless people on the street corners in Sedona. What was my next plan? I was obsessed with making the story perfect. Obsessed!

After almost two hours of driving around, I went to EightHundred-85. I tried to hide in the back, unseen. Unnoticed. Kendra saw me. There was no way she would remember me from the night me and Leigh Anne stopped in.

Or did she?

I left quickly and returned to my hotel.

Or did you?

In my room, with the help of Jack Daniel's, I said, "What the actual fuck, Jason." Not a question. A statement of fact. What the actual fuck was I thinking?

"No one ever got away with murder" was the first thing that my rational brain finally said. When I reached the bottom of the bottle, I realized no matter what I wrote, no matter what order I organized my thoughts and words, no matter what anyone criticized, what I wrote was perfect. My book was my world that I created. If I wanted to write the sky was green, then the sky was green. It was my world. Anyone who read the book must live in the world that I created.

I owed my friend Jack my life. At least I thought I did. I thought Jack saved me from making the biggest mistake of my life. Now, tonight, alone in my room, while my husband sleeps in our bedroom, I questioned all my life's decisions.

If I didn't have to get up early tomorrow, I would call up ole Jack and see if he wanted to hang out tonight.

CHAPTER THIRTY
JASON SHAW

The next morning, without telling Benjamin where I was going, I got in my car and drove the hour and a half to Flagstaff. It was a peaceful drive. The scenery changed from the cacti I loved into the mountainous evergreens I loved to visit. It had been a long time since I made that drive. I sat in my car for 20 minutes before I worked up the courage to go inside.

"I'm here to speak with Detective Harris," I said.

The lady behind the desk looked up from her screen. I obviously had interrupted something she was doing.

The building was quiet and practically empty. I guess I was expecting a room filled with hookers, drug users, and wife beaters all waiting to have their rights read to them before someone took them away to their cells. That was what I get for watching too many police dramas on television.

The lady at the desk instructed me to have a seat and wait. The chair was hard. The area was sterile, for lack of a better word. Not like a hospital where you felt a clean, chemical feeling, but sterile as in lifeless. The waiting room in a funeral home had more life than the waiting room at the police station.

Moments later, I saw a tall, scruffy-faced man walk around the corner. He wore denim and a plaid button-up shirt, nothing like what they wore on *CSI*. He extended his hand and offered his introduction.

"Jason, I am Detective Nathanael Harris. You can call me Nate. I do sincerely want to say thank you for driving up here to meet with me on such short notice."

"I'm doing what I can to make this go away as fast as possible," I said.

He led me to a room down the hall. All I could hear were our footsteps. The sounds were loud, almost as if each of us were wearing high heels. I noticed his limp. It caused the echos of our shoes to be offbeat: one, two, and, three, four, and, one, two, and, three, four, and. We passed several closed doors and finally stopped at a room labeled "Interrogation Room B." In the center of the room was a rectangular table with three chairs surrounding the table. A detective was already seated in one of them. There was, what I assumed from my TV shows, a two-way mirror on one wall. My imagination ran wild as I thought about who might be on the other side listening and watching.

"This is Detective Baker," Detective Harris nodded towards the officer already in the room. "You knew this day was coming," Detective Harris started. "I am sure you are smart enough to know I have done all my research. I have crossed every t and dotted every i. There is no sense in filling this room with anything other than the truth."

"I understand," I said.

"I want to start by reading your rights," Detective Harris said.

"My rights? Am I being arrested?"

"No, I just want to be clear that you know you have rights, and I want to be clear on what your rights are," he said. "You have the right to remain silent and refuse to answer questions. Anything you say may be used against you in a court of law. You have the right to consult an attorney before speaking with me and have the right to have an attorney present during the questioning now or in the future. Do you understand the rights?"

"Yes," I said.

"Would you like an attorney present during today's questioning?" Detective Harris asked.

"No," I said.

"How long have you owned The Golden Bones?"

"About eleven years," I said. I noticed his right index finger tapped his knee.

"How did you come up with the name?" Detective Harris asked.

"It started out as a retirement home for dogs. When people retire, society refers to that time as the Golden Years, so I wanted to have a play on words," I said.

"Clever," Detective Harris said. "You said, 'started out as a retirement home for dogs.' What is it now?"

"It's everything, still a retirement home, but also a hospice. It's a pet cemetery for those who wish to bury their pets. I also can cremate pets and make memorial items for the pet parents to keep."

"Sounds interesting," Detective Harris said. "How did you get into that line of work?"

"I have a degree in mortuary science, but I just didn't enjoy it. I wanted a job doing something with animals. I did some research and found there was a need for the services I offer, and after a few years of struggling, here I am."

Detective Harris' thumb slightly pointed up. Baker's eyes noticed the movement, and she wrote something down.

"Tell me about the incident at the Tattered Cover?" Detective Harris asked.

"I was just sitting there, then some lady came up and asked why I killed her sister," I said.

"Maybe a little more detail in your explanation," Detective Harris said.

"I was there on my book tour. My publisher had set up several stops around the country that I would visit to promote my book. Everything was going as expected. This was not the first stop on the tour. My first stop was a shit show, excuse my language."

Detective Harris nodded.

"My first stop was a mess," I said. "I didn't know what to expect. I wasn't prepared for the amount of people. Hell, I didn't even know what to write in the books that people were expecting me to sign! Anyway, by the time I arrived in Denver, I felt like a pro. I had thought of something creative to write when I signed the books. I wasn't nervous anymore, even though I don't like crowds.

"The doors of the bookstore opened, and the people started to come in. I did a quick reading and some introductory comments. I did my best to show each and every person my gratitude and appreciation for not only buying my book but coming out to meet me."

I glanced at the mirror and noticed Detective Baker's eyes were on Detective Harris' fingers. What were they doing?

"A few minutes into the signing, this girl asks why I killed her sister." I said. "And that's really all that I know."

Detective Harris stared back. "Did you recognize her?"

"No, I had never seen her before." But I did recognize her. From where, I couldn't remember—at first.

Detective Harris' left index finger bent slightly, making it gesture down.

"What was your initial thought when she made this allegation towards you?" Detective Harris asked.

"My first thought was, 'Who is this crazy lady?' Then I was hoping there was a security guard near," I said.

"What can you tell me about Charli?" Detective Harris asked.

"What?" I asked.

"Did you notice anything unique about the girl?" Detective Harris said. "Tattoos, birthmarks, you know, anything that would make her stand out?"

"If it weren't for that video being plastered all over the internet, I don't think I would even be able to tell you what color hair she had."

I began to fidget in the hard plastic seat. This one is harder than the one in the waiting room.

That's what she said.

"You seem a little nervous," Detective Harris said.

"I'm under investigation for murder!" I said. "Of course, I'm nervous. I get nervous talking to the cops in QT when they hold the door open for me when I get my morning coffee. But don't mistake my nervousness as anything other than that, just nerves."

I tried to smile to show my sincerity.

189

"How much do you weigh, Mr. Shaw?" Detective Harris asked.

"180 something," I said.

"I've looked through your laptop and notebooks," Detective Harris said. "I've found some very interesting things."

"I'm sure you did. So I will just ease your mind by saying, yes, there are many searches around the subject of murder. I did a lot of research for the book. Of course, since I've never actually murdered anyone, I searched how to do it so I could properly write about it."

"Yes, that's one of the things I wanted to talk about, but I'm also curious about another topic that was frequently searched," Detective Harris said.

He opened a file and pulled out multiple screenshots from my laptop. "Why so many searches for strip clubs in Flagstaff?" he asked. "Specifically, why did you search for EightHundred-85 multiple times?"

"I'm a curious individual," I said.

"That doesn't answer my question," Detective Harris said.

"Actually, Detective, it does," I said. "I'm sure you know, there are many unusual searches on my laptop. Many things that the average person might never lookup. Murder, strip clubs, wholesale cremation supplies, Brazilian fart porn. Like I said, I'm a curious individual. I'm always researching things. I don't keep myself glued to my phone like many people. I am, however, addicted to my laptop, and I am addicted to Google."

"I am glad you brought up the cremation," Detective Harris said. "Would it be a problem if I came down to look around The Golden Bones?"

"Why would that be a problem? I'm going to cooperate with you fully because I have nothing to hide," I said.

"Here is what I think happened," Detective Harris said. "You were writing your book, doing the research that you refer to, and decided you wanted to see if the research was real. I think you wanted to see if you could get away with murder. You drove up to the Flagstaff area one night, picked up Francine Platt from EightHundred-85, drove her to a campground, and murdered her."

"That's absolutely ridiculous!"

"It will be your turn to talk in a minute," Detective Harris said. "Right now is your time to listen. After you killed her, I am just curious as to why you didn't take her back to Phoenix with you and cremate her?" He paused. "I mean, don't get me wrong. I am glad you didn't because that would have made it really hard for me to solve the case."

"Well, for one, it's against the law to cremate a human in the same retort that is used for animals," I said.

"Murder is also against the law," Harris interrupted.

"And two, I didn't take her back with me because I didn't go to Flagstaff. I didn't pick her up from a club, and I didn't kill her," I said.

The left index finger bent again. I noticed Baker made another mark on the notepad.

What is he doing with this fingers?

I ran my hands over my head. The short hairs felt rough.

Oh, Jason, you are just damning yourself even more. The fidgeting is a dead giveaway that you killed her. If we are going to get away with this, you must sit there, look him in the eye and answer his questions. Don't get angry.

"How did you decide on who it was going to be?" Detective Harris asked.

I didn't say anything.

"Is it possible that you accidentally killed her?" Detective Harris asked. "Maybe you and Franki were hanging out at the club, a few drinks in. She asked you for a ride home. Things got a little steamy in the car. Maybe she thought you wanted to go a little farther than she did," Detective Harris said. "You are an attractive man. I am sure she saw that too. What if she made some advance on you, and you panicked? Maybe pushed her off of you just a little too hard? She hit her head on the window of your car and blacked out. You didn't know what to do next. You turned off the main road and ended up in a deserted campground. She came to, and then you just stabbed her. You lost control and just stabbed her."

I shook my head violently. I was so angry. Tears wanted to form.

Do not cry.

"Baker, can you go grab Detective Travis for a second? I think we are going to need another witness," Detective Harris said.

She left the room.

"OK, Jason, right now it's just you and me," Detective Harris said. "Be honest with yourself. We all know what happened. Baker and Travis will be back real soon to

192

document your confession. Just make this easy on all of us."

Seconds later, the door opened. Baker came back with the other detective. Baker sat down, and Detective Travis stood in the corner.

"Now, go ahead," Detective Harris said.

"There is nothing for me to 'go ahead' with," I said. "I did not kill that girl! I didn't kill her on purpose, and I didn't kill her on accident. She did not die because of me or because of the book I wrote!"

All three of them stared at me.

"I believe you said I have the right to remain silent?" I asked. "I'd like to use that right."

With that, Travis left the room. Baker grabbed the notepad and followed him. Detective Harris stood up.

"I will show you out," he said. "But I will be in touch with you real soon."

I got back to my car. A little over three hours had passed since I had left my house this morning. I powered on my phone.

Benjamin: Where are you?

Benjamin: Hello?

Benjamin: I tried calling, it went to voicemail. Call me!

Leigh Anne: What's going on? Ben just reached out to me. Call me

I called Benjamin right there in the parking lot of the police station.

"Where are you?" he asked.

"I'm in Flagstaff," I said. "The police wanted to talk to me. So I drove up this morning."

"And you didn't bother letting me know?"

"You didn't bother to say 'goodnight' last night," I said. I'm sure there were better words I could have chosen. I softened my tone and tried again.

"You were sleeping, and honestly, I'm still upset over our discussion from last night."

Benjamin was silent.

I was silent for a moment, too.

"And by your lack of response, I can tell you are still upset over it, too," I said.

"When are you coming home?" he asked.

"I'm leaving now," I said. "I should be there before dinner. Should I pick something up for myself, or will you be cooking? It would be nice to sit down and have a meal and a civilized talk."

"I can cook. I'll see you soon," he said.

"I love you," I said.

"I love you, too."

I pressed the red button to hang up.

It's funny, I still said 'hang up' even though I hadn't actually hung up a phone since I was ten years old.

On my drive home, a few things started to fall into place in my head. I recognized the woman because she and her sister were twins. I don't know why I didn't put that together until now. Leigh Anne and I saw Kendra dancing at EightHundred-85 when we went to Flagstaff for our weekend writing retreat. I didn't tell the detective that's why I looked up EightHundred-85 so often. I wanted to see if eventually a random photo of her might end up on their webpage.

I got lost in my thoughts about why my brain had a hard time knowing that Kendra and Franki were the same person.

Franki, twin sister of Charli.

Kendra, stripper.

Franki.

Kendra.

Marshmallow.

Nicole.

Marshmallow would have corrected me about using the word stripper. I hadn't spoken to her since this whole mess started. Why hadn't she called to check on me?

My mind wandered.

How did this happen?

I just could not wrap my head around why the book was so similar to the actual murder.

Maybe I did do it?

You did it.

Maybe I got so wrapped up in my head, and I actually did kill that girl. The mind can do some crazy things. Was it possible that it was blocking the memory of what I did?

I killed Franki Platt. I went to the hotel, got drunk, killed a girl, wrote down what I did, and called it fiction.

Did you?

The pine trees began to disappear in my rearview mirror.

I arrived home just before dark. Benjamin had dinner ready. Complete with candles and calla lilies.

"I just want to start off by saying I'm sorry," he said.

"I'm sorry, too," I said. "I understand this is hard on you, but you will never understand the amount of stress this

195

is putting on me. I will tell you one last time, and I don't want to ever have to repeat it again: I didn't kill Franki Platt." I said that with about a 50% certainty in my mind but 100% conviction in my voice.

I don't believe you.

We enjoyed our dinner. Let me rephrase—we had our dinner. Trust me when I say it wasn't a typical dinner. There was an awkward tension in the air. Almost as awkward as the way the word awkward was spelled. Our conversation was not free-flowing; it was as if I was in another interrogation. This time, my husband was asking the questions, and I was giving the textbook answers.

We slept in the same bed that night, but the space between us was filled with doubt, mistrust, and the unknown.

CHAPTER THIRTY-ONE
CHARLI PLATT

The past few weeks had been odd. Sometimes when I was out, people recognized me. At the advice of my family, I had declined all interview requests, even to my boss at the paper, which made work weird. My dad thought we should make a public appearance together once and then be done so he bought me a plane ticket to come home.

My flight from Denver to Phoenix was thankfully uneventful. I didn't mind flying. Today, by the blessings of the plane fairies, the seat next to me was empty. My dad picked me up in Phoenix. We grabbed some lunch at my favorite BBQ joint by the airport and then made the drive to our home in Winona.

"We are going to the TV station tomorrow at three," my dad said.

"OK. Have you talked to anyone yet, a lawyer, maybe?" I asked.

"No, there's no need," my dad said.

"What do you mean there's no need?" I asked.

"That guy is guilty," Dad said. "We know it, he knows it, the media knows it. Tomorrow is our chance to tell the rest of the world."

"I understand that. But there is no way this is going to just end with an interview on local news. I think you need to call a lawyer just to get the ball rolling," I said.

"They think I did it," Dad said.

"What?"

"The police think I did it," Dad said. "They called me in for questioning."

"They called me, too," I said. "I think that's normal."

"At the end of my interview, he asked me if I played any part in Franki's death."

"Why would they even think that?"

"I don't know," Dad said.

"Even more reason I think you need to call a lawyer," I said.

"We will see what happens tomorrow," my dad said.

The majority of the drive home was silent. We had some small talk about work, the family, and basic life stuff. I talk to my parents often, so we didn't have a lot to catch up on. When the pine trees came into view, I knew I was home.

I had not been back since I moved. My parents had been to visit me, but honestly, I had been scared to be home. My mom was waiting in the yard to greet us. She gave me the biggest hug I can ever remember. Dad carried my luggage in and left it in the living room. We all went into the kitchen for a brownie and a big glass of milk.

"I just pulled them out of the oven," Mom said.

She knew they were my favorite. I finished my milk and went towards my room. Our room. I walked down the hall and stood at the door. My knees weakened. I could feel my cheeks starting to flush. Flashes of memories came flooding back.

"Mom, Charli won't let me wear my pink sweater," Franki yelled.

"I told her I was going to wear it when we talked about it yesterday!"

"I hate you," Franki yelled.

"I hate you, too."

I turned the door handle and slowly walked in. Nothing, and I mean absolutely nothing, had changed since the day I left. When we were ten years old, we decided to combine our separate rooms into one room where we slept and one room where we played. Our Jack and Jill bathroom connected each of the rooms. Our bedroom had two matching twin beds, two matching nightstands, and two matching desks. Franki used the closet in the bedroom. When you walked through the bathroom into our playroom, you found a television, complete with a Nintendo Wii so we could play 'Just Dance,' two mismatched bean bags, a small sofa, and my grandma's rocking chair. My closet was in that room.

When I was 10, the monster in my closet would always scratch at 1:53 a.m. each morning. It did that for two months. One night I asked Franki to sleep in my room with me because she didn't believe me. That night, we laid in my bed both promising not to fall asleep. At 1:53 a.m., the monster scratched. We got up, went to Franki's room, and slept safely together through the night. The next morning we came up with the idea of sharing Franki's bedroom and making my room the playroom. When we got older, we renamed the playroom to our relaxing room.

I never heard the scratches from the closet again.

"There is nothing in your closet," Mom said.

"Mom, there really is! I heard it too," Franki said.

"For the safety of BOTH of us," I told her. "It really is the only option."

"If we do this, you will both be responsible for keeping both rooms clean," our mom said. "None of that, 'she made the mess, so I am not cleaning it' nonsense that you have said in the past."

"Thank you, thank you, thank you," we repeated in unison as we group hugged our mom.

I sat down on my bed and stared at Franki's. I tried to hold back my tears but then realized, why? Why do I have to hold back my tears? I was sad. She was gone. I was in our room, and she was gone. I didn't have to hold back anything.

Tears fell. One by one. Two by two. Twin trails running down my cheeks. I wiped them with my sleeve. I laid down on the bed, wrapped my arms around my Hannah Montana doll that still called my bed home.

"Slow down," our mom yelled.

Today was our seventh birthday. Mom made us wait in the house while everyone else settled into their chairs in our yard. Balloons, streamers, flowers, and rainbows decorated every square inch of our yard. It was finally time for us to make our grand entrance. The doors opened, and we ran. We ran down the dirt trail that lead from our back porch all the way into the woods.

"Happy Birthday," everyone yelled!

This birthday was a special one for us. We were turning seven on the seventh, which meant it was our Golden Birthday. Mom told everyone this year was the year not to buy us matching gifts. She gave us a 30-minute speech about how when we open our presents, even if we don't like them, we must pretend that we do. She also explained that we would not be getting the same gifts as we had in the past. Every birthday we would open up two shirts that matched or two new dolls that were exactly the same. One year, my aunt gave us scarves she knitted. They, too, were exactly the same.

When you were twins, especially under the age of 10, every birthday was the same. One of two things happened. One, someone gave us one gift and said, "It's for the both of you, so share." Or two, we each got one of the exact same things.

"It's a Hannah Montana doll," I exclaimed!

"I hope I got one too," Franki said.

We opened presents one after another, both feeling the joy and excitement of double the amount of toys. Today, we each got 19 different presents, not 19 doubles of the same thing. To us, that meant we got a lot of gifts that year. I still remember the last present Franki opened.

I think everyone at that party will always remember.

"Why is she black?" Franki asked as she opened her Bratz Doll.

"The lady at the store said girls played with Bratz because they were all different colors," my aunt said.

"Well, I'm white," Franki said. "I only play with white dolls. TAKE IT BACK!"

Mom was furious. "Franki, what did I tell you?"

"I don't care what you told me, Mom," Franki said. "I am not going to pretend to like a black doll."

And then Franki left our party. She went to her room, locked the door, and wouldn't come out for the rest of the day. She even missed out on our birthday cake.

That was the last big birthday party we ever had. The rest of them were small gatherings of family. The presents turned back into doubles or shareable gifts.

I wiped my eyes and went into the relaxing room. I sat on Franki's beanbag. When we were 15, Franki jumped on her beanbag chair. She hit it so hard and caused it to explode. Those tiny white beans flew everywhere! Our mom was never able to find the same one again. Those mismatched bean bags were the start of us becoming individuals.

"Oh, my God! What are you going to tell Mom?" I asked.

"Obviously, I have to tell you you did it," she said. Franki just laid there on the deflated bag laughing.

"You wouldn't dare," I laughed.

"Mom, Charli busted my bean bag," she yelled.

There was a knock on the door, bringing me back from my memories.

Mom pushed it open. "You doing OK, kiddo?" she asked.

I looked up. She brought me tissues.

"I still have some bad days," I said. "I guess being in our old room brought so much back."

Mom sat on my beanbag. "That's why nothing has changed since you left. I don't like coming in here."

"I'm sorry I left you and dad. I thought it was the only way I could heal. It was selfish," I said.

"No, kiddo, it was the healthiest thing you could have done," Mom said. "But I'm glad you are here now."

"How are you and Dad holding up? Honestly," I said.

"You two were always and will always be daddy's little girls. Your father is not allowing himself to heal," she said.

"And you?"

"I'm healing, but that doesn't mean I'm not heartbroken," Mom said. "What about you? How are you?"

I sat there, not wanting to answer the unanswerable question. When someone dies, it's everyone's first instinct to say, "I'm sorry for your loss," and then ask how you are doing. The first month after my sister's death, I would get angry every time someone said, "I'm sorry for your loss." It's like the cashier telling me, "Have a nice day." You're not really sorry, and they don't really care if I have a nice day. It's what society has programmed us to say, and thus it means nothing anymore. I'm sorry for my loss too, but that doesn't bring her back, and it doesn't make me feel better. It took me a long time to stop focusing on the phrase and to focus on the sympathy behind it. I went to sleep one night, and in my dream, Franki said to me that I didn't lose her even though she is dead. She told me she is with me every day and therefore she couldn't be lost. From that moment on, whenever someone said, "I'm sorry for your loss," I just started replying with, "I didn't lose her. She's just not here." It became my way of saying thank you for your concern. Thank you for your empathy. Thank you, thank you, thank you.

"Every day is different," I began. "Some days, I'm doing well. Some days I can't get out of bed."

"I have those feelings, too," she said. "I tried going to a support group, but as you know, everyone here knows everyone's business, so instead of support, it was just people sitting around feeling sorry for themselves while actually only there to be nosy and get the gossip from everyone else.

"I just really feel bad for your father," Mom continued. "I think, overall, I've allowed myself to heal, and he just keeps forcing himself to suffer. He constantly tells me it's his fault it happened. When he talks in his sleep, he says, 'I'm sorry for doing this to you' over and over."

"Have you asked him what he's sorry for doing?" I asked.

"Yes, but he says he can't remember his dreams. I made him go see a therapist. He went regularly for about three months and then stopped. He said the therapist wasn't doing anything but making things worse."

"Typical reaction from Dad," I said.

"You know your father. If he can't fix the problem himself, then there's nothing that needs fixing," she said. "That's almost a direct quote of why he stopped going."

"He's taking a nap," I said. "He will never even know."

Franki and I "borrowed" dad's truck three days after we had gotten our license.

"You drive," Franki said. "I just know I'll crash into a tree or something."

"You drive for a mile," I said. "And I will drive for a mile."

That agreement worked. We were going down the road, windows down and radio turned up, not a care in the world until a porcupine walked—not ran—across the road.

"Look out!" I screamed.

Franki slammed on the brakes and laid on the horn, but the porcupine stopped right in front of the truck. Franki swerved to miss it and drove into the ditch. When the truck came to a full stop, we opened the doors and ran to inspect the damage. As we got out, the porcupine started running straight at us! It seemed as if he wanted to get this revenge on us or the truck. We both got back in, shut the doors, and rolled up the windows. That is, we tried to roll up the windows, but they wouldn't budge. I climbed into the driver's seat to drive us out of the battle zone. When we got home, we walked around the truck. There was not a scratch anywhere, thankfully.

I made Franki tell dad that we were sitting in the truck listening to the radio. We told him we rolled the windows down, and they wouldn't go back up. Dad went outside, did his best mechanic's inspection, and said, "Well, at least we won't get snow for a few more months."

205

We looked at each other, knowing that was his way of letting us know we broke it, he can't fix it, and he would just leave the windows down all summer long.

"How do you feel about the interview tomorrow," I asked Mom.

"I think it's at least going to help get the story back in the public eye again," she said. "You know how quickly the news stopped talking about it. If the news isn't talking about it, then the community isn't talking about it. If the community isn't talking about it, then the case isn't getting solved."

"Do you really think JD did it?" I asked.

My mom sat there before she began. "No, I do not. I haven't read his book, and I don't want to read it. But I just can't see how someone could take the life of an innocent girl just to write a book."

Mom got up and left the room. I went back to the bedroom. I would always cherish the millions of memories we made in this room. I could never forget them. They were continually creeping back into my mind. Ghosts from the past were here to haunt me again. I laid down and closed my eyes. I forced myself to fall asleep before more memories made me fall apart.

CHAPTER THIRTY-TWO
CHARLI PLATT

We arrived at the news station at 2:40 p.m. "Early is on time, on time is late, and if you are late, just go home." That's the motto my dad had used his entire life. Our interview was not going to be live, thankfully. I spent most of my morning going over the 'rules' we learned in journalism school about preparing for a television interview. I helped both my mom and dad select their outfits. They kept with their personal style but fit the "stick with solids, no greens, white, or black" rules my professors would consistently tell us.

Dad led the way into the building, followed by Mom then me. This was not my first time in the KNAZ studios. We had several visits to the studio during school to give us examples of real-world experience. We were greeted and then taken to a room and were told to wait. We sat down on the lush leather seats and stared at each other. The seats were cold. Very cold.

The producer came in promptly at 3:00 p.m. She sat down and explained the entire process to us. While we were not doing a live interview, we would not be doing multiple takes. We had one shot at answering the questions. The interview would be shown that night during the evening broadcast. The producer handed my dad a list of questions that would be asked to give us time to prepare ourselves. He also told us not to assume Tracey would limit the questions to the ones on the paper. After 15 minutes of dos and do nots, the producer left the room, informing us we needed to be on the set in 30 minutes.

"I will do the majority of the talking," Dad said.

"Remember, be pleasant. Keep eye contact with Tracey," I said.

I looked at Mom. "Don't tap your foot if you get restless or nervous."

"We are here for Franki," I said to my dad. "Please don't turn this into the start of a lynch mob."

"Oh, princess, you know my temper is as bad as yours," Dad said. "You already went off on that guy, and now I'm going to ensure the world knows we are here to fight."

I pulled out my phone to pass the few remaining minutes before we went to the set. I opened my daily news app, and there it was. "Listen to this," I said. "Best selling author JD Shaw has been taken into custody."

"Oh my God," Mom said.

I clicked on the article and read it aloud, "Phoenix police, in partnership with the Flagstaff PD, arrested Jason Daniel Shaw this morning on suspicion of his involvement with the 2018 murder of Francine Platt of Winona. After Charlene Platt publicly made a recent accusation of Shaw, the Flagstaff PD assembled a team to refocus on the cold case. Francine Platt was found brutally murdered in April 2018. After two months of the once ongoing investigation, no arrests were made, and the case became listed as cold. Sources indicate that recently discovered evidence has led to this arrest. Shaw's arraignment is set for tomorrow at 9 a.m."

The article was posted less than an hour ago.

"Well, they will definitely be focusing on that during this interview now," Mom said. "You can just toss those questions into the trash," she said as she pointed to the list the producer left us.

"Just remember, do not say anything bad about JD," I said. "If this goes to trial, we don't want to start off looking like the bad guys. This interview is about Franki, not him."

I'm still new to the media industry, but I'm not naive. I know how it works. We have to keep ourselves in a positive light. We are the victims. We are not the monsters.

We were led to the set where we were formally introduced to Tracey Lynn. She would be doing the interview. She took turns, shaking each of our hands as we all were seated. I admit I was a little starstruck.

"I know this might be difficult, but remember why we are here. Justice has not been served. I'm hoping by having you here today, we can put a little pep in the detectives' step to solve this case!"

She doesn't know yet, I thought to myself. How have they not told her about the arrest? Did I read it wrong?

Everyone took their places. The lights were bright. The seats were comfortable. The cameras were aimed directly at us. The teleprompter was cued up.

"In five, four, three, two," the producer pointed to Tracey.

"Tonight, we are joined by the Platt family. Their beloved daughter and cherished sister was brutally murdered just 14 short months ago. After many weeks of investigation with no leads, little evidence, and no suspect, the case went cold," Tracey said.

The words continued to scroll.

"Gary, Monica, and Charli Platt are here to share, in their own words, what it's been like over the past year waiting for an answer, waiting for justice, waiting for their closure."

She paused, made brief eye contact with each of us, and then returned her gaze to the camera.

"What they don't know is moments ago, an arrest was made in conjunction with the case. Author Jason Daniel Shaw was taken into custody on suspicion of his role in the murder of Francine Platt."

I immediately knew I had to speak up before my father could. This was a classic journalist's trick to take the interviewee by surprise. "A surprised interviewee is more likely to give honest, newsworthy answers." I always paid attention in school.

"We actually read that about three minutes before we got to the set," I said. "We are glad that he has been taken into custody, and we are looking forward to justice being served."

"If I were to ask you if JD did it, what would your response be?" Tracey asked.

I jumped in before my dad could speak. "As a family, we have our opinions that we are not ready to share, but I can say this, the past year has been one of heartbreak, sorrow, loneliness, and eventually healing. We just want to be able to go to sleep at night knowing that the person who did those horrible things to my sister is caught so they cannot do these things to another innocent person."

Tracey could tell that I was going to take charge of the rest of the interview. She could tell I was not going to slip up and let my emotions get in the way. She turned her focus to my parents.

"Monica, what was it like when you heard the news of your daughter's murder?" Tracey asked.

"It's something I would never wish on anyone. Having your child ripped from your life instantly in a senseless act of—of murder is the worst thing imaginable," Mom said.

"Gary, what's the one thing you would like to say to JD?" she asked.

"I hope the crazy son of a bit-" my dad started.

"DAD!" I interrupted.

"I'm sorry," Dad said. "I hope my daughter's murderer is found and prosecuted to the full extent of the law."

Tracey went on asking more questions, but I think she could tell we were not going to say anything that would make for good TV. The entire interview lasted about seven minutes. When it aired tonight, I was sure someone would edit it down to three. Who knows what would actually end up on the viewers' screen.

We loaded up in Dad's old blue Ford truck to head back home. The truck had been in the family since before Franki and I were born. Its roof was rusted, the seats were cracked, and it looked as if it were held together by a wing and a prayer. But he was eventually able to get the windows rolled up! My dad loved this truck. He called it his thinking truck. Dad made all of his important decisions in this truck. "When I was ready to ask your mom to marry me, I drove around in this truck for three hours," he had told us once. Franki and I both learned to drive in this old truck.

It was so crowded when dad wanted all four of us to go for a ride in the mountains. Now, without Franki, we seemed so far apart.

When we got home, I went straight to our room and called Gwendy.

"JD's been arrested," I said.

"I know, it's all over the news. They are even showing snippets of your interview already."

"What!? We literally just walked in the house from finishing up the interview," I said.

"This is big, Charli, this is big! What do you think is going to happen?" Gwendy asked.

"I don't know. I mean, I don't know." I said. "It's just I didn't think anything would ever get fixed... not fixed... I guess I mean..."

I sat there for a few more seconds.

"I feel like all my emotions are coming back up that I had either buried or processed, and they are just getting dug up and ripped to shreds again," I said.

"I can't even imagine what is going through your head," Gwendy said. "How is your dad doing?"

"He's doing as well as I would expect him to do. He is angry. He got called in for questioning again. They asked him if he did it!"

"No way!" Gwendy said.

"Yes, way."

"What did he say?" She asked.

"According to him, he just got up and left and said the interview was over," I said.

"That's crazy!"

"I know," I said. "I'm guessing they have been interviewing everyone since the case got reopened."

"Well, you know me and my conspiracy theories. I wasn't going to tell you, but that was one of the conspiracies I read about. So people are already making that assumption."

"There are conspiracy theories about my dad and my sister?" I asked.

"Among other things. Just stay off Reddit so you don't upset yourself. I'll keep you up to date with the good ones as they unfold," Gwendy said. "And I know they will unfold."

"OK, thanks. I'm going to see what I can find out about the interview. I'll text you later. Love you," I said.

"Love you, too," Gwendy said.

I sat on the side of my bed and opened the browser on my phone. I needed to see the clip Gwendy said she saw. A few keywords and a tap here and a tap there, and I saw it.

"Tonight, we sit down with the Platt family whose daughter's unsolved murder recently surfaced again, all from a murder allegation her sister made about a best-selling author," said the voiceover.

They cut to the cell phone footage. "Why did you kill my sister?" I yelled.

"Her family was torn apart after the murder of one daughter. Their other daughter fled the state as she could not bear to be with her family. Find out their side of the story tonight!"

Fled the state? That made it sound as if I was the one who killed her! I had never liked that side of the media. I can guarantee it is not something that was taught in school. There was never a class called "Over Exaggerating The Truth To Cause Panic" or "How Do We Jumble Words to Make Things More Confusing So No One Ever Really Knows the Truth." And now that I think about it, I didn't even say anything about moving to Denver at all.

I decided not to tell my parents about the footage. I can only hope they don't edit it into a drama filled clip that makes us end up looking like the bad guys.

CHAPTER THIRTY-THREE
JASON SHAW

I spent the night in the cell alone, thankfully. The last thing I wanted to have to worry about was sharing such a small space with a stranger who did something horrible.

You did something horrible. Maybe they are glad they are not in here with you.

"Get up," the guard said, "you have a visitor."

I did as she said.

"Turn around, place your hands behind your back, and slide them through the opening."

I did as she said.

She led me down the hall to an even smaller room.

"I'm Rusty Cooper," he said. "This my assistant, Carlisle. Your father sent me."

"My father?" I asked.

"Yes, your father," Rusty said. "I have been following the developing news very closely. He, your father, hired me to represent you in court."

Rusty was a young man, no more than 30 years old. Tall, thin, and in possession of a killer mustache. His red-rimmed glasses sat perfectly on the bridge of his nose. Carlisle was older, her early 50s. She had a mustache as well, just not nearly as defined.

"You're going to fix this mess?" I asked, skeptical. Don't judge a book, I thought.

"I would like to talk to you for a while and see what you and I can come up with," he said. Rusty sat down and held his open palm towards the seat opposite him as a gesture for me to sit as well. "I'm an Arizona native. I'm a recent graduate of South Texas College of Law. Carlisle has worked for the firm for 15 years. She's the best damn paralegal this side of the Mississippi. I think this will be an open-and-shut case."

He spoke in a very straightforward, no-nonsense monotone. There was a slight southern twang to his speech.

"I've spent the last 48 hours working with my mentors, pulling everything we could find about the case. We were afraid you would be arrested, so we wanted a head start," Rusty continued. "I'd like to review it all with you today, as well. The only thing missing is you. I would like to get started immediately if you are comfortable with my representation at the end of our conversation."

"If you want my honesty, I need yours too. Why choose to represent me?" I asked. "And how—why did my father get involved?

"Those are fair questions," Rusty said. "I have never been to trial before. This would be my first case. I graduated with top grades. I'm confident in saying I'm book-smart, now I need to apply my knowledge."

"So, I would be your guinea pig?" I asked.

"I would rather call you my first client," he said. "If you don't mind. And with the expertise that Carlisle will bring, you will be in great hands."

"Well, Mr. Cooper, I will say that I have nothing to hide. I have done absolutely nothing wrong. So I will take you up on your offer to represent me."

I hope he's good. You don't want to rot in prison.

216

"And my dad? Did he also discuss payment with you?" I asked.

"Yes, he and I have settled the details of that aspect already," Rusty said. "My dad and your dad were old Army buddies, I recently found out. While I've never met your dad, he trusts my dad, and therefore he said he trusts me."

He extended his arm across the table, and we shook on it.

"First, I do not want you talking to anyone about anything, not your husband, not your friends, not other lawyers, no one. Just me and Carlisle. If anyone and I mean anyone wants to talk to you, I must be present. That especially applies to law enforcement," he said.

"OK," I agreed.

"Second, you must be honest with every question I ask you. Even if it's information that will condemn you, you must be honest," Rusty said. "My job, as your lawyer, is not to believe if you are innocent or not. My job is to make the jury believe that you are not guilty."

"I'm innocent, so OK," I replied.

"And finally, you must trust me in every possible way. If I tell you to do something or say something, you must trust that it is for a reason."

"OK," I replied.

"Not a man of many words, are you?" Rusty asked.

"I'm still trying to process everything," I said. "I guess there's just not much to talk about."

"There is more than you can imagine," he said. "Carlisle, want to start reviewing what we know?"

"Absolutely," she said. "I've pulled together media interviews, police records, and crime scene photos." She pulled multiple folders from her bag. "And finally," she reached in one last time, "this." A copy of *She Loves Me Not* was tossed in the center of the table. Multiple PostIt notes peeked from the pages of the book.

Your book.

My book.

We are going to start at the beginning. This is the very first article that we were able to find. She handed me a photocopy.

Missing woman found, dead.

Local woman, Francine "Franki" Platt, aged 23, of Flagstaff, was found brutally murdered. While parking their vehicle before they began a sunrise hike, Bear Cannon and his wife, Summer, noticed smoke rising from behind the restroom. Bear said his first thought was, "Some idiot didn't put out their campfire." He went on to say, "I needed to [urinate], so I decided to [urinate] on the fire to help put it out." Bear then explained that when he rounded the corner, he saw a woman hanging on a charred cross. Flagstaff PD was immediately notified and responded to the scene. Detective Michelle Baker had the following to say, "During this active investigation, we are asking any individuals who may have been in the vicinity of Wild Burro Gorge over the past week and might have seen something, anything, please contact us at the Flagstaff PD."

Francine Platt is survived by her parents, Gary and Monica and her sister Charlene.

"This was printed in on April 10. A few days after she was found," Carlisle said. "Have you ever been to Wild Burro Gorge?"

"Yes, I used to go camping there when I was a kid," I replied.

"Any recent trips?" Rusty asked.

"Yes," I said. "I don't recall the exact date, but my friend, Leigh Anne, and I stayed at a motel for a weekend getaway in that area last year."

"Oh? Why did you pick that area?" she asked. "Out of all of Arizona?"

"We went to write." I picked up my book. "I wanted to be away from the distractions of the city. I knew the area was pretty, and I hoped it would inspire us…me to finish my book."

Carlisle scribbled down something onto her notepad.

"What was the name of the hotel?"

"I don't remember, but there are only three motels in that area," I said. "It's the last one before you get to Winona."

"I'll look into it," Carlisle said. "Gary, Franki's father was, at one point, a suspect as well. We will do some more digging, but we know that he increased the life insurance policies on both the girls a few months before Franki's death." She grabbed another sheet of paper and skimmed, reading only the highlights aloud. "Gary Platt, 58 of Winona, AZ, has been under the microscope, blah, blah, blah." Her eyes continued darting across the page. "Ah, here we go…Sources have told us that he, Gary, was the easy suspect. The entire family knew of the insurance increase, which lessened [the undisclosed detective's] suspicion. I checked into the insurance agency as well. They are a private company. The agency is owned by Gary's brother." She looked up and continued talking. "It turns out Gary's brother had recently gone through a divorce, and his ex took him for everything he had, except the insurance agency. Gary took out such a large policy as a favor to his brother. Large policies equal large income for his brother."

"That sounds like there's really no reason to suspect him then," I said.

"To the untrained eye," Rusty said. "But to me, I think it's an avenue we are going to still pursue."

"Take a look at the coroner's report. Read it carefully," Carlisle said. "Tell me if you notice anything suspicious. She handed me the paper.

CORONER'S REPORT
EXTERNAL EXAMINATION:
At 7:30 a.m. on April 4, 2018, the autopsy began. The body is presented in a black body bag. The victim is completely nude with no jewelry or accessories. Earrings and bracelet were found near the victim. Burns covered the entire left lateral side of the body and minor abrasions on the right side. The cranial hair was singed in connection with the body burns.

The body is that of a normally developed white female. It is measuring 66 inches and weighing 108 pounds. The appearance is consistent with the estimated age of 23. The body is cold and not embalmed. The right eye is open while the left eyelid has been scorched to cause it to remain closed. The irises are brown. The pupils measure 0.3 cm. The hair is dark blonde with lighter blonde highlights and brown regrowth that measures 1 cm, wavy, layered cuts, and approximately 13 inches in length at the longest point.

A sharp force entry was found on the left side of the chest between Rib 3 and Rib 4 (known throughout this report as entry A). A second sharp force entry was on the left posterior of the chest cavity (known throughout this report as entry B). Entry B impaled the scapula.

A sharp force entry was found on each arm between the ulna and radius. The entry in each arm is 9/16 in circumference and enters in the collar wrist and exits in the dorsal wrist. A sharp force entry was found near the talocrural joint of each leg.

Upon examination of the skull, blunt force trauma is seen on both the maxilla and the mandible. This trauma has caused all teeth to be absent from the victim's mouth. No dental records will be able to be obtained.

The victim has level 5 fingertip amputations on all ten digits. The wounds are consistent amongst all 10. Multiple lacerations are found on the right and left forearms (defense wounds). A tattoo that says 'False hopes __ than fears' on the inside right wrist. Puncture wound destroyed the center of the tattoo.

Wounds (trauma and sharp force entry) appear to be inflected by a right-handed person.

INTERNAL EXAMINATION:

HEAD—CENTRAL NERVOUS SYSTEM: The brain weighs 1,198 grams and within normal limits.

SKELETAL SYSTEM: Observations of a shattered maxilla and mandible made. Multiple facial fractures are found.

Fragments of bone have penetrated the brain tissue. The left scapula is scraped due to Entry B.

RESPIRATORY SYSTEM-THROAT STRUCTURES: The oral cavity shows trauma, as stated above.

The lungs weigh: right 355 grams; left 362 grams. Entry B is a single point of entry; however, the internal trauma shows two tracks entering the chest cavity.

CARDIOVASCULAR SYSTEM: The heart weighs 249 grams, below the normal weight. Penetrating trauma was isolated to the left ventricle. The right ventricle was ruptured. The left and right atria were intact.

FEMALE REPRODUCTIVE SYSTEM: Examination of the pelvic area indicates the victim had not given birth and was not pregnant at the time of death. There is evidence of recent sexual activity but no indications that the sexual contact was forcible. Vaginal fluid samples are removed for analysis. The breasts have silicone implants, which I removed for identification purposes. A serial number REF-204 LOT 305123 was imprinted on the left. A serial number REF-204 LOT 305109 was imprinted on the right.

DESCRIPTION OF INJURIES – SUMMARY

Blunt force traumatic injury with multiple cranial fractures resulting in craniocerebral injury. The injury appears to have resulted in multiple blows administered to the anterior of the head. The subject had puncture wounds in both wrists and ankles. Subject was alive when puncture wounds were administered. Lack of smoke inhalation indicates the subject was postmortem when the fire was started. The trauma wounds resulted in cardiopulmonary arrest.

Drug Screen Results:
Urine screen {Immunoassay} was NEGATIVE.
Ethanol: 0 gm/dl, Blood (Heart)

Ethanol: 0 gm/dl, Vitreous
Clive Michaels, Ph.D.
Chief Toxicologist
April 4, 2018

EVIDENCE COLLECTED:
1. One (1) 8 inch fixed blade chef's knife.
2. One (1) partially burned book of matches.
3. Two (2) silver hoop earrings.
4. One (1) silver bracelet.
5. Four (4) 6 inch railroad spikes.
6. Samples of Blood (type O+), Bile, and Tissue (heart, lung, brain, kidney, liver, spleen).
7. Fifteen (15) swabs from various body locations to be tested for the presence of hypochlorite.
8. Eleven (11) autopsy photographs.
9. One postmortem CT scan.
10. One postmortem MRI.

OPINION
Time of Death: Body temperature, rigor and livor mortis, and stomach contents approximate the time of death between 7:30 and 9:30 p.m. on April 1, 2018.
Immediate Cause of Death: Cardiopulmonary arrest
Manner of Death: Homicide
Remarks: Decedent initially presented to this office as a homicide victim. Upon completion of the autopsy, I submit my agreeance.
Witnesses: Detective Michelle Baker of the Flagstaff Criminal Investigation Division
Sharon Ans, M.D.
Coconino County Coroner's Office
April 4, 2018

"Notice anything odd in the report?"

"No, not really," I said.

"Look here," Carlisle said. She pointed to the report where it said one wound was made in the back, but it hit the scapula. Further down the report, it said the wound in the back caused two paths of trauma to the lung. She explained that the two paths meant the killer pushed the knife in, pulled it out slightly, and then jabbed in back in at a different angle. "How would it cause lung trauma if the shoulder blade stopped it from going all the way in?"

"I'm still not understanding your point," I said.

"Something seems wrong with the report," Carlisle said. "Almost as if someone altered the report or intentionally overlooked a key piece of evidence."

I glanced at my book.

She loves me.

She loves me not.

How many petals must fall before you learn the truth?

We sat there and discussed everything. And I mean everything! The interview with my lawyer was more intense than the interview with the detective. And, just like with the detective, I gave them the honest truth. I even told Rusty about the voices in my head that were telling me things. I hadn't shared that with anyone yet.

"Oh, that's good information," said Rusty.

"Why?"

"If your mental health is in question, we can start the case with not guilty by reason of insanity," he said.

"I'm not guilty, and I'm not insane," I said.

224

"You just told me about the voices inside your head telling you that you killed someone," Rusty said.

"Yes, because you said I needed to trust you and tell you everything," I said.

"Exactly," Rusty said. "That means we can lessen your sentence with that plea."

"Or, you can just do your job and prove my innocence in a case that I am actually innocent." The volume of my voice continued to rise.

"OK, OK. I think we're off to a good start," Rusty said as he stood up. Carlisle followed his lead. "I'll be in touch with you real soon."

He reached in his briefcase. "I cleared it with the guards, and I brought you some books to help you pass the time."

"Thank you," I said. That was probably the best thing he could have given me today.

That afternoon in the cell was another lonely, quiet one. I looked through the small stack of books Rusty brought me and selected the shortest book in the pile. I knew my attention span would be wavering. I don't remember much of what I read. I don't remember when I fell asleep.

"Let's go!" yelled the guard. "You know the drill."

He startled me awake. Did I sleep all night? I got out of bed, walked to the bars, and turned around. He cuffed me through the hole in the bars, and we walked down the hall, where I met Rusty.

"I've got your bail hearing set up for today, in one hour," he said.

"Bail hearing? You think they are going to let me out?"

"No, I don't, but it's part of the process," Rusty said. "You just need to present yourself as a well-spoken, well-mannered member of society."

"I can do that," I said. "What's going to happen there?"

"It's a straightforward and quick process," he said. "We walk into the room, state our facts, and the judge will make their decision based on what they feel are the best determining factors."

"And those factors are?"

"Who knows?" Rusty said. "It's more of a gut feeling, I think. There isn't a checklist or a grading scale when it comes to things like this. Let's hope we get them during a good mood."

I returned quickly to my cell, brushed my teeth, and tried to make myself appear to be well put together and not stressed.

By the time we arrived at the court, my mind was all over the place. I still could not wrap my head around the speed at which things were happening.

"All rise for the honorable Zachary Justice," said the bailiff.

I leaned over to whisper to Rusty. "The judge's last name is Justice?"

He shushed me.

Rusty did his first job really well. After a short statement from him and a few questions from Judge Justice, I was a free man. Well, not free. It cost me a lot of money to post bail. A lot! But, now, I could wait for my trial in the comfort of my own home. I had to surrender my passport, and soon I would be the proud owner of a nice ankle monitor so they could keep track of my whereabouts.

Benjamin was waiting for Rusty and me when we got home.

"It took a lot of work, but I was able to convince the judge to let him out on bail," Rusty said.

"What? How?" asked Benjamin.

"He's a local business owner with strong community roots," Rusty said. "He has no previous offenses. Not even a speeding ticket—which is pretty impressive."

I nodded.

"How much?" Benjamin asked.

"$250,000," I said.

"Holy shit!!! Where did that money come from?" Benjamin asked. "Never mind, that's not important. I'm glad you're home."

Rusty reminded me to stay home. I was not to leave my porch. One step onto the ground, and the alarm would immediately alert the authorities. I would be treated as if I were a runner. Apparently, running away while awaiting your trial was frowned upon.

Rusty left. My husband and I went inside.

"I need you to look me in the eye," Benjamin said. "You look me directly in the eye and tell me you didn't do it. I need to hear that from you."

"I have told you before, and I will tell you one more time. I did not kill that girl.

"I thought you would be a little more excited to see me," I said. "Are you still going to hate me after the trial is over, and I am a free man again?"

"I don't hate you. Honestly, I don't know what emotion I feel, but this is just too much for me to handle," Benjamin said.

"Too much for YOU to handle? What? Staying at home, like normal? Going to work, like normal? Cooking a meal whenever you want, like normal?" I asked.

"Meanwhile, I've spent the last two days sleeping on a hard twin mattress and eating food that tastes like frozen leftovers from six years ago. I haven't been able to go to work in, hell, I can't even remember the last time I went to work. So don't you dare stand there and tell me this is too much for you to handle."

Benjamin's expressionless face was his usual face of submission.

"I'm sorry," I said. "I just really hoped I would come home, have a nice dinner, hang out, and then go to bed."

"I'm sorry, too. I'm sorry that this is happening to us. Not to you, not to me, but to us." He paused. "And I'm sorry that I am scared to be around you. There, I said it. I'm afraid of you, Jason."

"Why would you be afraid of me? What have I ever done in my life that would make you fear me?"

"I am just scared," he said.

"You really think I killed that girl."

His lack of response told me my answer.

"Well, sadly for you, I cannot leave this house. So, I guess if you don't want to live with a murderer, you will have to leave."

"I know," Benjamin said, "I think I will."

He did. It was the last time I saw him for a very long time.

CHAPTER THIRTY-FOUR
JASON SHAW

I awoke the following day to a knocking at my door. I grabbed a shirt and answered the door. It was Rusty and Carlisle.

"I hope you got some rest last night," Rusty said. "We've got a lot to go over today."

Before I could answer, Rusty and Carlisle had set up shop on the dining room table. "I was able to get copies of some of the crime scene photos," Rusty said. "I'm going to need you to think like a detective today, Jason. Anything out of the ordinary that you see just might be something that someone else overlooked. It might be the one thing that saves you from prison."

A pretty boy like you will be popular in prison.

"These are pretty graphic," Carlisle said. "You need to be prepared." She handed me the first one.

I looked at the photo of the girl's body. Perfectly hung on an imperfect cross. The cross was leaned against the back of the concrete bathroom. The shingles on the edge of the roof had burnt off, and the grass around the base of the cross was gone.

"Oh," I sighed while staring at the photo. I had seen a lot of things during my schooling and my career, but nothing quite like this. She had large nails driven through her wrists, one in each arm. There was one nail driven through each of her ankles. The four nails held her body. She looked... Christ-like.

She looked like D'Arcy did in your mind.

"The remaining photos are not as graphic but might prove to be more important."

Rusty handed me a stack of photos: a shoe print, tire tracks in the dirt, a used book of matches, and a knife. My knife. My expression must have shown something.

"What is it?" Rusty asked.

"This looks like my missing kitchen knife," I said. "Follow me."

The three of us got up and walked into the kitchen. I pointed to my knife block with one knife missing. Rusty pulled one of the steak knives out and compared it to the chef's knife in the photo. Same brand, same color, same set.

"OK, well, this is interesting," Rusty said. "What happened to the knife?"

"I don't know. It went missing a long time ago. I always assumed Benjamin had lost it or thrown it away without telling me," I said. "He has a short temper sometimes, and I wouldn't put it past him to throw it away if it wasn't sharp enough. That's just how he is."

Carlisle went back to the table to grab her phone. She returned and took a picture. We all three went to sit back down. "I have studied all of the interview files already," she said. "It just seemed so odd that no one saw anything—no witnesses to the abduction, no witnesses to the fire, nothing. According to the files, everyone loved Franki. Her family said there was only one person who they knew of that should be a suspect. Joseph 'Joe' Montez." Carlisle shuffled through the stack of papers and pulled out a photo of him. "Franki had filed a restraining order against him the previous year. He was harassing and stalking her during the time she lived in Phoenix when she worked for a place called Scout's Honor."

Another panic set in. I've been to Scout's Honor many times. Why am I linked to so many things?

"According to the statements, he was why Franki left Phoenix and returned home," she said. "The file showed he had a strong alibi. He was on vacation in Rocky Point, Mexico, from March 29 until April 4. His credit card statements, cell phone records, social media, and witnesses all corroborated the information. In his personal statement, he said he had not seen or spoken to Kendra, Franki's stage name, since she left Phoenix."

"Do we have current contact information for her old employer at EightHundred-85 or Scout's Honor?" Rusty asked Carlisle. "We might be able to get some information or maybe a character witness from someone."

"I know that once the word got out about one of the strippers being murdered, EightHundred-85 couldn't keep any employees," Carlisle said. "They closed about three months after the incident. I'm sure I can locate the previous owner and maybe some of her old co-workers."

"Dancer," I said. "They call themselves dancers."

Carlisle ignored my correction. "Now, another interesting thing that I found, the interview tape with Gary went missing. The transcript was also incomplete. Someone had removed some things."

"That is interesting," Rusty said. "I wonder what that means."

"I asked my contact, and they couldn't give me much more detail than that," she said.

Rusty grabbed the pile of photos and flipped through to get the one of the tire tracks. "This is where it gets a little tricky," he said. "After all of the police analysis, the tracks at the scene were made from three sources. One, the hiker's truck; two, the forensic team's van; and three, the department's police cruiser."

"So there were only three sources of tire tracks and very little footprints?" I asked.

"Here," Rusty said as he pulled out the photos of the footprints.

"So there were little to no footprints at the scene and only three unique tire treads. Isn't it odd?" I asked. "I mean, how can you kidnap a girl, nail her to a cross, burn the cross, and leave no tire marks?"

How did you do it?

"It rained pretty steadily for two days before the day we believe she was murdered. That would have washed away anything there prior to April 1," Carlisle said. "My source said they searched the surrounding areas and found a few ATV tracks, but they were all on trails in the woods around the campground. None of them lead near the crime scene. My source said they assumed the killer, or killers, had taken the cross to the site a few days before. Those footprints and tread marks would have then been washed away. The night they took Franki to the campground, they would have laid out multiple tarps to…," Carlisle said, "to carry out the process. They found little blood splatter, no debris, and, well, overall, there was just no mess."

"Where are Franki's footprints?" I asked.

"Great question," Carlisle said as she pulled out some other photos of the scene. "Look right here. There is a small footprint that we can assume is Franki's. It's just a heel impression that's cut off halfway. That's where they assumed the tarp ended," she said. "You have to remember, she was a tiny lady. And even in the mud and rain, she wouldn't have left much of an imprint."

Rusty paused thoughtfully. "If the murderer was so careful to prep the scene and left little to no blood splatter or forensic evidence, why did he leave the knife?"

"Exactly!" Carlisle said. "It was purposefully placed there. My opinion? He was hoping it would be found."

"But why?"

Why did you leave the knife, Jason?

Carlisle grabbed another sheet. "The knife is sold at various retailers throughout the country. There's no way to track it down to one retailer specifically. Why a kitchen knife? It doesn't seem like it would be my first choice as a murder weapon. And why a knife anyway if he had the nails?"

"I agree," Rusty said. "It's almost as if he was going to kill her with the knife, and the crucifixion was an afterthought. They don't seem to be consistent with any criminal profiles we have."

"And the book of matches?" I asked.

"Nothing special," Carlisle said. "They are found at almost every convenience station in Arizona."

After what seemed like hours, the two left. They said I was helpful in providing the information about my missing knife. Other than that, I didn't think I provided any other information or assistance. Carlisle really seemed like she knew what was going on. Rusty, I still wasn't sure how I felt about him.

PART 3

January 2020

CHAPTER THIRTY-FIVE
JASON SHAW

THE TRIAL

Day 1

The case had become one with such high public visibility that there were no open seats left in the courtroom. National and local news crews lined the streets. Protestors for both sides filled the designated free speech area. "Justice for Franki" signs were equally distributed amongst signs proclaiming my innocence. #rightthewriter was trending on social media. The country had tuned in to see what would happen to JD Shaw. Sales for my book were unimaginable. Those who read the book had blogged, submitted reviews, and overall created enough free marketing that the publisher was hard-pressed to keep up with the demand. Even those who hadn't read the book and had no desire to read the book were buying it. Social media's power to make you think you need to own a part of current events that will become a part of history was impressive.

I sat at the long table with Rusty, mindlessly picking at the invisible lint on my pants. I didn't want to look around the room. I knew all eyes were on me, and I knew there were eyes I didn't want to see.

The judge opened the door from his chambers that led into the courtroom. He was a tall, plump man. His hair was dyed black, too black for someone his age.

"All rise," said the bailiff.

Everyone stood.

"The District Court for the state of Arizona is now in session. The Honorable Judge Charles Warren presiding," said the bailiff as the judge took his seat.

"You may be seated," said Judge Warren as his eyes glanced across the room. "Jury members, please stay standing."

The bailiff walked to the jury, "Please raise your right hand. Do you affirm that will listen to this case and render a true verdict and fair sentence based on the evidence presented in this case?"

They all repeated, "I do."

"You may be seated," said the bailiff. He walked toward Judge Warren and handed him a stack of papers. "Your honor, this is case #12-33215, State of Arizona v. Shaw."

He skimmed through the papers and directed his attention to the jury once again. "Members of the jury, you have been assembled today as part of your civic duty. The Constitution provides all citizens the right to a fair trial by a jury of their peers. Your duty during this trial is to determine whether the defendant, Jason Shaw, is guilty or not guilty based on the facts and evidence presented here in the courtroom." He turned his gaze towards the prosecutor. "Mr. Finn, are you ready?"

Marcus Finn stood, "Yes, your Honor."

"Mr. Cooper, are you ready?" asked Judge Warren.

"Yes, your Honor," he replied.

Judge Warren nodded, "Mr. Finn, you may begin."

Marcus Finn was a short man, no more than 5'8". He was dark-skinned. I thought he was possibly Hispanic descent. His eyes were black. There was no dividing ring where his pupils met his irises. His neatly combed hair framed his square jawline. The spattering of grey hairs made him look sophisticated and respected. He wore red shoes, the same color as Rusty's glasses. They showed everyone he was not afraid to make a bold statement.

"Ladies and gentlemen of the jury," Marcus began, "you have been given a job. Part of the duties of this job is to listen. You will listen to truths." He paused. "And, you will listen to lies. Your job is to understand the difference. On April 2, 2018, the body of Francine Platt was found. She was disposed of in the middle of the woods. She was stabbed, bruised, mutilated, crucified, and set on fire." He turned his body slightly but never broke eye contact with the jury. "Jason Shaw is the cold-blooded murderer who did those horrific things to that young lady.

"That's the truth.

"What would make a man like Jason Shaw kill a random stranger? The evidence will show he is of sound mind. The evidence will show he is passionate about being perfect. The evidence will show that while researching for a novel he was writing, he couldn't find exactly what he wanted. He couldn't find any information on the emotions a person feels when they kill someone. He took the research into his own hands—his own bloody hands. He selected a victim, killed her, defaced her body, and wrote about his experience. While his novel is considered by many a work of fiction, I will prove with sound evidence that it, in fact, is a work of non-fiction.

"Your job is to interpret the facts. Your job is to ensure justice for Francine Platt is served."

Francine. Franki. Kendra.

He turned around and headed back to his seat. Marcus had been practicing law for 13 years. He had won, according to Rusty, 89% of his cases. Marcus sounded confident. He spoke with conviction, and as he did, the 12 strangers in the jury box did not break eye contact once.

I could hear Rusty mumble, "Here we go" under his breath as he stood.

"Good morning, ladies and gentlemen of the jury. My name is Rusty T. Cooper. I am here today representing my client, Jason Daniel Shaw, better known as JD Shaw, to most of the country."

His slight southern drawl was stronger today. Spending time in Texas had given him a subtle twang. His nerves made it more audible. "We are here today bringing you the facts in the case. These facts will show you a story. A story about fame. A story about truth. A story about lies. A story about murder."

Rusty momentarily broke eye contact with the jury and looked at me. "My client is a relatively new published author. A man, who a few months ago, no one knew. A man who spent the past year and a half of his life writing and publishing a novel. A fictional novel. It seems..." He paused. "It seems there are some people who think it is a retelling of a murder. I admit the parallels to the novel are similar to real life. Yes, it is true, Jason did kill someone." He paused again. "He killed a fictional character in a book that he wrote. That is the only fact that matters in this case."

He spoke in a straightforward, almost rehearsed speech. Each word was chosen deliberately. Each word was said with purpose.

"During this trial, you will hear from my client. In his own words, he will tell you about his life. He will tell you about the experiences of writing his fictional novel. He will tell you how he is wrongly accused of murder," Rusty said.

"You will hear from the prosecutor's witnesses. They will try to convince you that my client is guilty. They will fill this room and your heads with lies. My burden of proof is to provide enough evidence that Jason Shaw did not kill Francine Platt. That's my only job. Your only job is to determine who is right and who is wrong."

Rusty returned to his seat, sat down, and looked at the judge.

Marcus began to present his side to the jury. He called his first witness to the stand. Most of what he said was a blur. He called so many people to the stand that morning— friends of mine, family of Franki, police officers of Arizona.

I recall seeing Detective Baker, Detective Harris, and multiple other police officers that I didn't recognize. What they said, I don't know.

The morning was a blur.

The afternoon was a blur.

"I do not recall if he was there."

"Yes, I am the one who initially did the interview."

"He killed my niece."

"It wasn't his blood mixed in with Francine's on the knife."

"Yes, a knife similar to the one found in Jason's home is what was used as the weapon."

The words that were said became jumbled with who said them.

"They were leaving home for college. I just wanted them to be safe."

"My name is Nicole Jones, but Marshmallow is my stage name."

"There is no industry standard for that."

Person after person. Witness after witness. Rusty asked follow up questions when it was his turn. I sat there feeling scared. I was confused as to how this all happened. It was never-ending.

"Ladies and gentlemen of the jury," Marcus said as he headed towards his laptop. "I present to you the murder weapon." Marcus projected a photo of a knife onto a screen for everyone to see. Soot from a fire had blackened the blade of the knife. The fire had severely damaged the handle, but I recognized what remained. It was from the same set I had at home.

Marcus then split the screen and projected the forensic report.

"Ladies and gentlemen, this report clearly states that multiple fingerprints were found on this knife," he said as he pointed to the screen. "This knife was used to kill Francine Platt. This knife has Jason Shaw's fingerprints on it."

A collective gasp came from the room.

Jason... Jason...Remember that night when you went on your UFO tour. You never went on that tour... remember.... your plan. Your plan was to kill someone.

SHUT UP, I silently screamed back at this voice inside my head.

The voices were loud. Louder than they ever have been. What was happening to me?

I leaned to whisper into Rusty's ear. "You've got to say something."

"No, I don't. This is the part where they are trying to prove you are guilty. We knew about the knife. I know what to say when it's my turn to speak," Rusty said.

See Jason, even your attorney doesn't want to help you win. You killed someone. You will be punished.

Marcus continued, "I want to warn you, the next slide is going to make you uncomfortable, but I feel it is important that you see." He pointed the clicker towards his laptop and the image on the projector changed. "Ladies and gentlemen, these are the five railroad spikes that were used to crucify Francine Platt."

"After Francine was murdered," Marcus said, "she was nailed to a cross with these nails you see here. Her wrists were ripped open by these nails. Her ankles were shattered by the nails. In a final act of 'research,' Jason nailed Francine to a cross."

I don't know how long Marcus stood before the court presenting evidence.

I don't know how long I had a conversation with this new voice in my head.

I don't know...

243

A full eight hours we sat in that courtroom. The rigid chairs creaked with every move I made. It became evident that I wasn't good at sitting for long periods of time. I continually shifted in my seat to try to find the exact spot that would keep my comfort level at its highest possible setting. Nothing worked.

I was relieved when Rusty said it was over for the rest of the day.

CHAPTER THIRTY-SIX
JASON SHAW

The Trial

Day 2

Yesterday Rusty had informed me that today would be centered around our evidence. Today we would tell our side of the story. We would tell our truth. We would plant the shadow of doubt in the jury members' minds.

I wasn't sure that Rusty believed me, still. I thought his entire defense was based around the shadow of a doubt.

Rusty stood. "At this time, your honor, I would like to call Jason Daniel Shaw to the stand."

The room was silent as I stood up. I looked at the jury with a blank expression on my face and then headed towards the stand. My penny loafers clicked with each step I took.

Click.

Click.

Click.

Click.

Click.

Click.

Click.

Seven steps from my seat to the witness stand.

Odd.

The bailiff swore me in. I had never been a religious man, but I prayed hard when my hand was on that Bible.

Rusty began. "Jason, can you tell me what inspired you to write *She Loves Me Not*?"

"Every year, I push myself to be creative," I said. "I never want to stop learning new things. I made a New Year's resolution many years ago to do something creative every year that I had never done before. I had never written a book, and I wanted to try it."

"Mr. Shaw," Rusty said. "Can you give us a brief summary of the book you wrote?"

"Sure. The main character, Denton, became obsessed with a store owner named D'Arcy. He fell in love with her, stalked her, and eventually kidnapped her. He tried to get her to love him, but she just didn't. One day she attacked him, and he accidentally killed her in an act of self-defense," I said.

"And by the end of the book, did he get caught? Was he convicted of a crime?"

"Yes and no. Not to spoil it for you," I said as I looked at the jury. "But the detectives show up, Denton sneaks out of the house and lays on D'Arcy's grave. The reader then assumes he killed himself."

"What was the experience like, if you had to describe it in just a few words?" Rusty asked.

"What experience?" I asked.

"The writing experience," Rusty said. "The concept creation. The execution of the concept. Formatting the novel. Those type of things."

"Most of the time, it was fun. Well, about 50% of the time, it was fun. The other times it was stressful. There was a lot of research. There was a lot of time away from my husband. There were fights between me and my husband; there were fights between me and my best friend." My eyes went directly to Benjamin's and then to Leigh Anne's. They were in the front pew.

"When you say fights with your husband, what do you mean?"

"Nothing crazy. We never got violent, if that's what you are asking. There were just times when some of the things I was researching would affect me," I said.

"What types of things would you research?" Rusty asked.

"The main character had some mental issues. I would look up various things that could be wrong with him. I wanted to ensure the book was accurate as possible," I said. "Symptoms, causes, cures. It's hard to explain."

"If you had to put a medical diagnosis on your character, what would you say best fit him?" Rusty asked.

"Anxiety disorder," I said. "That would be the main illness I associate with him.

"Does anxiety disorder cause a person to hear voices inside their head?" Rusty asked.

"I'm no doctor, but based on the research I did, I would say the answer is no," I said.

"Do you have an anxiety disorder?" Rusty asked.

"I've never been diagnosed with it," I said.

"Mr. Shaw, do you hear voices inside your head?" Rusty asked.

"Sometimes."

"Did those voices in your head ever tell you to kill Francine Platt, Mr. Shaw?" Rusty asked.

"No," I said.

Rusty walked to the desk and picked up a pen and paper. He showed the paper to be blank and handed them to me.

"Can you please print and sign your name on this paper for me," Rusty said.

"Objection," Marcus said.

"Your Honor, there is a reason," Rusty replied.

"Go ahead," Judge Warren said as he looked at me.

I picked up the pen and printed my name. Below that, I signed it.

"Let the records show, Mr. Shaw used his left hand to print and sign his name. I would like to read to you from the coroner's report. 'Wounds (trauma and sharp force entry) appear to be inflected by a right-handed person.'"

"Mr. Shaw," Rusty said. "Did you recognize the murder weapon Mr. Finn showed us yesterday?"

"Yes."

"Is it true that you own a set of kitchen knives like the one presented?" Rusty asked.

"Yes."

"And, is it true that one of your knives from your set was stolen from your home?"

"One of them is missing, yes, but I don't believe it was stolen."

"Do you believe it was your prints on that knife?" Rusty asked.

"Absolutely not," I said.

"As Mr. Finn told us, your fingerprints were allegedly one of multiple different prints on the murder weapon. Did you know there are over 150 ridge characteristics, or points, in your fingerprint? Take a moment, look at your thumb pad. I'll wait."

I noticed a few jurors looked at their thumbs while I examined mine.

"Did you also know there is no universal standard for the amount of those points that must match for the examiner to say two prints are the same? That means one examiner can match 10 points and say they are the same. Another examiner may say it requires 16 points for the prints to be a match. That means there are about 135 other points on your thumb that can be different for the examiner to say the prints match."

A few more of the jurors began to examine their thumbs.

"Eleven," Rusty said. "Eleven points were matched from Jason's left index finger to one print found on the murder weapon. That means there are about 139 points that did not match on the prints that were recovered from the murder weapon. While it is widely believed that no two people have the same fingerprints, it is a fact that eleven points on my fingerprints can have matching points on your finger," Rusty pointed to Carlisle. "And who's to say, even if it was Jason's print on that knife that he was the one who used it as a murder weapon?"

Rusty began to pace in the front of the room.

"Is it possible that someone broke into Jason's home, stole his knife, and used that to murder Francine Platt?" Rusty paused. His eyes scanned all 12 jurors. "Yes," he said as the answer to his own question.

Rusty and I went back and forth for a long time. I was relieved when he looked at the judge and said he had no further questions. Now came the hard part, Marcus. At least with Rusty, he had been able to prep me on the questions he was going to ask. We did a few role play questions about things he thought Marcus was going to ask.

Rusty sat down, sipped from his water glass, and watched Marcus head towards me.

"Isn't it true that you spent most of your free time researching your book?" Marcus Finn began.

"Yes," I said.

"I have some photo copies of things from your notebook," Marcus said. "Can you confirm this is, in fact, your handwriting?" Marcus showed me the sheet. I nodded in confirmation.

"For the record, Jason Shaw nodded his agreement that these pages are his handwriting," Marcus said. "Ladies and gentlemen of the jury, in his own words Jason has written the following. 'Ensure you have an alibi. Ensure you have a great disguise. Ensure you leave no evidence. Ensure the body can never be identified.'

"Those four things sure do sound as if you were planning on killing someone."

"Yes," I said. "Yes, they do. And, as you have stated, and my attorney has stated, and I have stated I wrote a book where someone was killed."

"Why would the main character of your book need any of these four things since his crime, as you put it, was 'an act of self-defense?'"

I sat there in silence, I didn't have an answer. I didn't know how to answer.

"Mr. Shaw, answer the question," Judge Warren said.

"My notes were filled with lots of things, ideas, concepts, drawings. It was my receptacle for all of the word vomit that would happen when I was planning. Sometimes I just needed to get ideas of out my head onto the paper. That's what those four things are. Word vomit." I felt like I wanted to real vomit.

"Can you describe, in detail for the jury, how you murdered the character in your book?" Marcus asked.

"In detail, probably not. It's been a very long time since I wrote it, and it's been a very long time since I have read it. D'Arcy attacked Denton. He got a pan, I think, and started hitting her as a form of self-defense. Then he strangled her with a rope, or maybe it was a chain."

"And after she was dead?" Marcus asked, "how did he dispose of the body?"

"He cut off her fingertips, broke her face with a hammer, maybe," I said. "Maybe it was a rock. He pulled out her teeth, and he crucified her."

Marcus asked, "And do you think it's odd that Francine Platt was disposed of in almost the same manner? Almost as if you wrote the scene exactly as it happened?"

"No, I don't find that odd at all. Mr. Finn. Have you ever read much yourself?"

Marcus didn't say or do anything to show agreeableness.

"One of my favorite book series is about a wizard named Harry. Harry Dresden that is, not to be confused with another famous wizard named Harry. In one of his books, there was a scene where a demon decapitated its victim and then sawed off both arms just below the elbow. The demon did this because he didn't want his victim

251

identified." I scanned the eyes of the jury. "That scene in that book, Mr. Finn, was my inspiration for the murder scene. That book was written in 2004, almost 15 years before I even decided I wanted to write a book. So, you see, Mr. Finn, my idea isn't all that unique or original. If you turn on any true crime documentary, you can find that what I wrote in my book has happened to hundreds, if not thousands, of victims. You are just trying to piece a story together to find a killer. I, sir, am not a demon, and I am NOT a killer," I said.

WOW, that was amazing.

"Why did you use five nails in your crucifixion?" Marcus asked. "During the research I did, most depictions of the crucifixion show the use of three or four nails, but never five."

"The fifth nail was the one that was supposed to be used to deliver the fatal wound to Christ," I said. "It was the nail that should have been put into his heart. According to legend, when the Romans went to get the nails from the metal worker, they only got four. The metal worker hid the fifth nail in an attempt to save Jesus and spare him his life.

"I wanted the fifth nail to be symbolic. I wanted Denton, the main character, to feel as if he followed the original plan set forth by the Romans, that D'Arcy might actually be resurrected for him."

Marcus was silent for a brief moment, then he continued. "What size shoe do you wear, Mr. Shaw?"

"Size nine," I said with a deep exhale.

Marcus had a projection of a photo, "This is a photo of a size 11 shoe print that was found at the site where

Francine's body was located. Isn't it possible that you could have worn shoes that are too big to ensure your prints were not found to be a size nine?"

"That's exactly what I would have done. As you stated earlier, my laptop was confiscated. That was definitely something that was found on my laptop as part of my research. But that's common knowledge, again, from watching any true-crime show," I said. "So to answer your question, anything is possible."

"Our records indicate that you stayed at Chrisholm Motel on February 26, 2018. Does that sound correct?"

"I'm unaware of the exact date, but yes, I stayed there once with my friend, Leigh Anne," I said.

"What was the purpose of that stay?" Marcus asked.

"Me and Leigh Anne had recently had a fight, and we were taking a trip to clear the air, make up, and move on. She and I also used that time to work on our novels," I said.

"What was the fight about?" Marcus asked.

"It was over Marshmallow," I replied.

"Marshmallows?"

"Nicole, Mr. Finn," I said. "We were fighting about Nicole Jones."

"I see," he replied. "During that trip, is that when you went to EightHundred-85?" Marcus asked.

"Yes, we did go there," I said.

"Is that the first time you had an encounter with Francine Platt?"

"It has been brought to my attention that yes, I, in fact, did have an encounter with her that night," I said. "But at the time, I was unaware of who she was."

"How many times after that night did you visit EightHundred-85?"

"I have never been back since that night," I said.

"Can you give me your thoughts on how a knife from your home that has your fingerprints on it was the murder weapon?" Marcus asked.

"I don't believe there is any evidence that proves the knife is actually from my home," I replied.

"Then how did your fingerprints end up on it?"

"I don't believe there is enough evidence that proves it is actually my fingerprint. You have said yourself, there are multiple prints that are definitely not mine also on that same knife."

Back and forth, we went. He kept trying to stump me with questions to make my guilt shine. I keep answering with truths that made me look innocent.

At the end of Marcus' cross examination, Rusty stood up, "Your Honor, I have one more question before I release this witness."

Rusty turned to the jury, "Ladies and gentlemen, I would like to read from the coroner's report a list of evidence that was collected at the scene. One 8 inch fixed blade. Mr. Shaw, didn't you list in your notebook that one of the steps to getting away with murder is to leave no evidence?"

"Yes," I replied.

"Do you think you would have forgotten to bring the murder weapon with you, assuming you killed someone?"

"No," I said. "I would definitely not leave the weapon behind."

Rusty continued, "One partially burned book of matches. Mr. Shaw, if you started a fire to burn the body and to help destroy the evidence, do you think you would have left behind a partially burned book of matches?"

"No," I said. "I would have ensured they burned completely."

Rusty walked back to his desk and projected the picture of the five railroad spikes, "Four six inch railroad spikes.

"According to the coroner's report, four railroad spikes were collected from the scene. Mr. Shaw, can you think of any reason the report says four spikes were collected, yet the photo from the police evidence shows five?"

I shook my head.

"I can," Rusty said. "Someone has tampered with the evidence. Someone is trying to set you up. Someone, who is probably in this courtroom, has altered the crime scene. They have altered the evidence. Someone wants you to go to prison for a crime they committed." Rusty stopped pacing, adjusted his tie, and looked at Judge Warren. "I have no further questions, Your Honor."

I returned to my seat. Rusty said he felt I did really well. He said that I told everything that needed to be told with conviction. Rusty told me he knew I was telling the truth, and he knew that the jury could tell as well. He also added that I needed to tone down my attitude a bit. I was trying to convince the jury I was not guilty. I was no longer trying to prove I was innocent. He reminded me those were two very different things.

"You're the good guy," Rusty said.

"I know, that's what makes me so frustrated," I said. "It's hard not to want to get up and punch him in the face."

"That's what he wants, Jason. He wants you to lose your temper. He wants you to punch him in the face. If you do, you've lost the case!"

Another day in court came to an end. With my usual escort, I made it to my car and headed home. I still found it odd that I was on trial for murder, yet I was just going home. Innocent until proven guilty, that's what they say.

CHAPTER THIRTY-SEVEN
UNKNOWN

"How did five nails get into the evidence photo?"

"I don't know, I guess I messed up."

"Yes, you really messed up! Now we gotta hope no one cares."

"We've gotten this far, don't lose hope now."

"False hopes are more dangerous than fears."

CHAPTER THIRTY-EIGHT
JASON SHAW

The Trial

Day 3

Judge Warren looked at the jury. "Ladies and gentlemen, the jury, both the prosecution and the defense have rested their case. Each attorney will now present their final arguments. While what they are about to say is not considered evidence, please continue to listen carefully and closely."

"Thank you, your Honor." Marcus looked at each juror. "Jason Shaw said he didn't kill Francine Platt. He said there was no motive. Ladies and gentlemen, that's what makes this crime so scary. If Jason had no motive for this crime, why does he need a motive for his next victim? What stops Jason Shaw from getting up from that seat, walking out of this courtroom a free man, and then killing another random stranger. He has no motive."

Every eye in the room was following Marcus' movements. He slowly paced from one end of the jury box to the other. He took small breaks to allow himself to speak directly to each of the 12 people. He returned to the lectern in the center of the room.

"As you leave this room, please consider the facts," Marcus said. "Fact. Jason's fingerprints were found on the knife. Fact. Jason's computer and personal notebooks showed months of him researching how to get away with murder. Fact. Jason made multiple documented trips to

258

Flagstaff and the surrounding area. Fact. These trips were used to stalk Francine Platt. These trips were used to plan the perfect murder. These trips were used to kill someone just to write what Jason calls 'an accurate murder' scene for his book."

Marcus stood confident at the lectern. "Jason makes his living from telling and selling lies. These lies are what make up the pages of his book. All fiction authors tell lies. That's what they are supposed to do. I can't fault Jason for telling lies. But remember, the lies in his book are re-enactments of the truth. The truth is he killed Francine Platt." Marcus finished his statement and returned to his seat.

Rusty stood up and began. "There is no way Jason could have killed Francine Platt. All of the evidence that has been presented has been circumstantial. You see that the prosecutor rushed to a conclusion and then tried to piece together their case. Not all of the pieces fit together, and there are a lot of gaps and holes left in their case. These gaps and holes in the prosecution's story are large enough to fill with reasonable doubt.

"The murder weapon is sold nationwide. Many of you may even have a set in your very own kitchen. Many of you may have one piece from your very own knife set missing. On that missing knife, from your set, is your fingerprint. Someone could easily have taken that missing knife from your set while you were at work. What would you do if someone stole your knife and used that knife to murder someone? Would you be responsible just because someone stole your knife?

"The fifth nail; Jason told us the metalworkers hid the fifth nail from the Romans to try to save Jesus from his terrible fate. Who stole the fifth nail from the crime scene? Someone did. Someone stole that nail, or spike, or whatever you want to call it. They stole it and yet, you know it was presented as part of the evidence. Did someone frame Jason? Was someone working against him all along?

"When you leave this room. If you have any doubt in your mind that Jason Shaw did not kill Francine Platt, you must submit a not guilty verdict." Rusty Cooper walked back to his seat and stood for a moment.

That's it? That's all he is going to say. You are going to prison, Jason. Get ready.

Rusty picked up a copy of *She Loves Me Not* and walked back to the jury. "I'd like to read a few lines from the last paragraph to you. 'Denton laid on the wet soil, the tears from the sky mingled with the tears from his eyes. His hands shook. His heart pounded. His voice quivered. His world would never be the same. He knew the light that D'Arcy gave him was gone. His light was now the only one left shining. He was afraid he would never find anyone else to compliment his light. What if the only way for D'Arcy's light to shine again was for his to go out?'

Rusty closed the book. "Do not let your emotions around the murder of an innocent woman outshine your judgment when it comes to the innocence of this man."

With that, Rusty pled my case. My fate and my future rested in the hands of 12 strangers.

Judge Warren began, "Members of the jury, you have heard all testimonies from both the prosecutor and the defendants. It is now up to you to analyze the information presented to you and determine the facts. You, and you alone, are now the judges of those facts. Once you have decided what the facts in this case prove, you must then apply the law as I give it to you to those facts as you find them."

"All rise..."

CHAPTER THIRTY-NINE
JASON SHAW

I received my usual escort to my home. I've had multiple police cars sitting at the end of my driveway since this whole trial began. I had been told it was for my safety, however, I knew it was more of a show of force for the rest of the community. No one wanted a murderer left alone.

Benjamin was home for the first time in a very long time.

"Are you going to stay here tonight?" I asked Benjamin.

"No."

"Are we finally going to talk?" I asked.

"Yes," Benjamin said as we walked into our living room.

"It's obvious to me whose side you are on. I wish it were mine, but I can tell that's not the case," I said.

"No matter the outcome of this trail, I don't think I can ever feel safe in the same home as you," Benjamin said.

"Why? What have I ever done to make you scared of me?"

"You are not the person I married," Benjamin said. "You have changed so much over the past year. You were always gone on your so-called writing retreats. When you were home, you were spending your free time at a strip club. You stopped going to work and just let your team handle everything. You changed."

"People do change, but that doesn't make me a murderer," I said.

"I'm not convinced you aren't," Benjamin said. "Your fingerprints were on the knife! The knife is the same one missing from our set."

"Don't get it twisted. A fingerprint. One. One print that is similar to mine was on a knife that is similar to ours. That's not proof," I said.

"It's just so hard, Jason."

"I'm still the same man you married. I didn't do it. I don't know what I can do to make you believe me."

"I just wanted you to know that our future is uncertain," he said.

"You've been gone for two months!" I said. "Of course it's uncertain. I'm on trial for murder. My future isn't certain."

"Good-bye, Jason," Benjamin walked out of the house. He closed and locked the door.

He's going to leave you.

"No, he's not," I said aloud.

OK, then when you are in prison, you will be leaving him.

"SHUT UP!" I said.

You shouldn't have done it.

"I didn't do anything."

How did it feel watching her die?

"I wasn't there, so I don't know."

Are you going to do it again?

My husband thought I did it, Franki's family thought I did it, the voice in my head thought I did it. You? Do you? Of course, you don't. You are the only sane person left that I can talk to.

I'm talking to myself.
I'm talking to you.
Maybe I am crazy.

CHAPTER FORTY
JASON SHAW

"Let the record show the presence of the jury, the defendant, and all counsel," Judge Warren began. "It is my understanding that you have reached a unanimous verdict, and this verdict has been handed to the bailiff."

Time stood still. Millions of eyes were upon me, not just those in the courtroom. People were protesting on the north side of the street with live coverage being broadcast to their phones. There were supporters with handwritten signs on the south side of the street. Some were armchair detectives at home who hadn't made up their minds if I was guilty or innocent. My lies were believable. My truths were not.

"The state of Arizona vs. Jason Daniel Shaw verdict," Judge Warren began. "We the Jury, duly impaneled and sworn to try the above-entitled case, unanimously find the defendant to the charge of first-degree murder guilty, signed floor person. Is this your true verdict, say you one and all?"

A unanimous yes was quietly said by the 12 members. The yes was muddled with smiles of accomplishment by some, and averted eyes by others. One man looked me directly in the eyes with sadness.

"The clerk will now ask each of you one question. Please answer yes or no," Judge Warren said to the jurors.

"Juror number one, is this your true verdict?" the clerk asked.

"Yes."

"Juror number two, is this your true verdict?"

"Yes."

"Juror number three, is this your true verdict?"

"Yes."

"Juror number four, is this your true verdict?"

"Yes," juror number four said, not with hesitation or questioning. But there was something in the tone of juror number four's voice. He was the last one I remember hearing. The clerk went down the line, one-by-one, asking each juror the same question. Each person answered with the same response.

"Members of the jury," Judge Warren said. "The court dismisses you and thanks you for a job well done."

I was led out of the courtroom in handcuffs. An innocent man condemned because of a book.

CHAPTER FORTY-ONE
CHARLI PLATT

"Juror number one, is this your true verdict?" the clerk asked.

"Yes."

Conner reached over and grabbed my hand.

"Juror number two, is this your true verdict?"

"Yes."

I intertwined my fingers with his.

"Juror number three, is this your true verdict?"

"Yes."

He squeezed.

"Juror number four, is this your true verdict?"

"Yes."

The Judge went down the line. Tears began to fill my eyes. I could also see my Mom and Dad holding hands. Gwendy sat next to Conner, tissues in her hand. I reached to grab one.

The trial had come to an end. My family and my friends sat there with me as we watched JD walk out of the courtroom. The shiny cuffs held his hands, showing no mercy. Providing no false hope that his freedom had not been taken.

My hand held—squeezed Conner's. My hand let me know that there was love left in the world. My hand showed someone else I was willing to let my past go and allow my future to be filled with love. My other hand held the tear-soaked tissue—tears of sadness, tears of relief, tears of healing.

My parents' hands intertwined. Their love, their loss, and their relief were held in their hands. When my father was first questioned as a suspect, his life changed. Even after JD was arrested, people talked. People whispered. Now that JD was going to jail, I hoped the town's rumors would stop and release my father from the imaginary prison everyone placed him in.

Gwendy's hand held one final tissue. She didn't offer it to anyone, but it was there if we wanted it. It was a reminder that it was OK to cry for as long as me and my family needed.

Her free hand came in to encircle me and Conner in a group hug. Our lives had been changed, each in different ways. The one thing that will never change is our friendship.

CHAPTER FORTY-TWO
NICOLE "MARSHMALLOW" JONES

"Baker here," she said when she answered the phone.

"We did it," said Nicole.

"We will talk more when I see you tonight, I love you," Detective Michelle Baker said.

False hopes are more dangerous than fears. I still remember seeing that damn tattoo every night she came to work. For whatever reason that quote stuck in my mind, it became my own personal motto. Hope. Kendra needed hope. I would never let her have that hope in the dance industry. Then when she starting calling me those names, saying all those racist things about me I knew she and I'd never be friends. She was the worst person in the world and I hated her. I wanted her dead.

I was thankful when she left Scout's. No one liked her. She moved back home to be daddy's little angel because she couldn't make it in the real world. She stole my money and vandalized my car. Most importantly, she tried to break my spirit. I never forgot it.

When I read Jason's manuscript and I saw he had put the quote as a thing that girl in the book said, I knew I could get away with it. I saw my perfect murder. I studied Jason's method he used in the book and pulled the best copycat murder the world has ever seen. I wanted to take it just far enough to make it a little different, but close enough to for readers to know it was the same. That's where the fire came in. I wanted to burn the bitch, light her up on a burning cross racist pieces of shits used to leave in black folk's yards. That would show her!

But in all honesty, I thought his book was shit and didn't expect anyone but me and that bitch Leigh Anne to ever read it.

I didn't even know this guy that well and he was telling me all his secrets. He was trying to be my best friend. I took advantage of the situation. It was part of my job, make the men think I like them and they give up more money. Jason was just another man that I made think I liked him. I was thankful when he invited me over for dinner one night. When he wasn't looking I stole one of his kitchen knives. That damn knife was so dull, I didn't think that bitch was ever going to die!

I knew she wouldn't meet me, so thankfully Michelle was able to go pick her up from the club in her police car. Michelle told her something had happened with her sister and she needed to come with her right away. Kendra believed her. Michelle drove her to the campground and we completed the task. When it was all said and done it was perfect. I thought Michelle had ruined the whole plan though with that fifth nail. She told me later that she saw it in the back of her patrol car and didn't read the reports. She put it into the evidence box and had forgotten about it til that lawyer brought it up.

I really was really rooting for him, though. Jason was a nice guy that didn't deserve to spend the rest of his life in prison, but neither did I. I was hoping they would find him innocent. I guess Jason wasn't that famous after all, but he's got one helluva story that will never let him be forgotten.

CHAPTER FORTY-THREE
JASON SHAW

I've sat in my cell with my cellie for three weeks. It took me those three weeks to learn that a gay murderer can share a cell with a straight bank robber just fine. It took me those three weeks to learn to refer to him as my "cellie" and not by his name. It took me those three weeks to learn that my life had changed forever. It took me those three weeks to convince myself I was not a murder.

Leigh Anne was the first person to come visit. We sat in the booth, the cold white phones in each of our hands.

"How ya doing, champ?" she asked.

"Well, I haven't been anybody's bitch yet."

She smiled, but it quickly faded.

"I'm just going to get this over with quickly and then we can talk about something else. Ben asked me to tell you that he's not coming," she said.

"He still doesn't believe me, I guess."

"No, he doesn't. He's also working with lawyers. He told me that he is going to sell The Golden Bones and then start the process of filing for a divorce."

"He can't sell my business!"

"He can. You are married so your business is also his business. And he knows you will be here for a very, very long time."

"It's OK to say forever," I said.

Tears began to form in my eyes.

"Do you believe me?"

"I'm here," Leigh Anne said. "My beliefs do not and will not impact me coming to visit you. Most importantly, they will not change our friendship."

"So that's your kind way of saying no," I said.

"That's my way of saying I'm your best friend, and I will come visit you every week until the day I die."

"I didn't do it."

"I don't want this to come across the wrong way, and believe me I've rehearsed several times about how to say this, so here it goes. You are not the only one whose life got fucked up by this. That family had to relive all of the issues that they had started to lay to rest. Your husband is wanting a divorce. And me, I've lost my best friend."

Her eyes looked down as she did her best to twist the metal phone cord in her hand.

"I no longer get to call you whenever I want. I no longer get to text you whenever I want. I no longer have you either," she said.

There was nothing I could say in reply.

We sat there for the remaining time and tried to make small talk, although most of the time was spent in silence. Comfortable silence that she and I had always been able to share. As we said our goodbyes and hung up the phone, I had to laugh. I actually hung up the phone for the first time since I was 10.

Acknowledgements

When I set out writing this novel, I never knew how hard it would be! (I also didn't know how to use parenthesis correctly and had no idea how much I loved an exclamation mark!) I never dreamt that the time spent typing away would lead to you holding this book. Without the support from my family and friends, this novel would still be an idea stuck inside my head.

Leigh Anne, there will never be enough Mister Bee Potato Chips in the world for me to say Thank You. You taught me so much over the past five years. The lessons will never be forgotten. Well, I'm sure they will be forgotten, but at least I have written a grammar lesson textbook from all of your notes and feedback that I can refer to in the future. Maybe I should publish that next? Thanks for all of our lunch dates, phone calls, video chats, and mail packs.

D'Arcy, thank you for allowing me the use of your name and being the muse to inspire the book within the book. Your love of true crime podcasts was contagious, I never imagined it would lead to this!

Jami, thank you for being my very first 'stranger danger' beta reader. You have no idea how long it took me to gain the courage to send you my draft. I just knew you were going to steal it and publish it as your own or write me back and tell me it's awful and no one should have to be put through the torture you went through of reading it! The feedback you provided was so helpful. I still look at your email with your notes, it made me cry (happy tears). I'm glad we became friends.

Daniel, I hope I become as famous as James Patterson. You were the first to tell me my book wasn't "your style." It was hard hearing that, but it gave me the realization that it won't be for everyone, and that's OK.

Thank you for your honesty, your notes, and your support. I did use some of your feedback to improve the story… don't sue me.

Finally, Jonathan. Thank you for all of your love, support, motivation, and always keeping the snack bowl full. You are always my biggest fan with any crazy idea I tell you I want to try (including this book). Hopefully, this book will become a movie one day so you will know what it's about. I love you!